Astrid Lindgren
Mio, My Son

Translated from the Swedish by Jill Morgan
Illustrated by Ilon Wikland

THE NEW YORK REVIEW CHILDREN'S COLLECTION
NEW YORK

THIS IS A NEW YORK REVIEW BOOK
PUBLISHED BY THE NEW YORK REVIEW OF BOOKS
435 Hudson Street, New York, NY 10014
www.nyrb.com

First published in Sweden in 1954 as *Mio, min Mio* by Rabén & Sjögren,
Sweden. This translation first published in 2003 by Purple House Press,
Lexington, Kentucky.
All foreign rights are handled by Saltkråkan AB, Lidingö, Sweden.
For more information about Astrid Lindgren, see www.astridlindgren.com.

Library of Congress Cataloging-in-Publication Data
Lindgren, Astrid, 1907–2002.
[Mio, min Mio. English]
Mio, my son / by Astrid Lindgren ; translated by Jill Morgan ; illustrated by
Ilon Wikland.
    pages cm. — (The New York Review Books children's collection)
Originally published in Swedish by Rabén & Sjögren in 1954 under title: Mio,
min Mio.
Summary: Young Anders is carried away from his bleak life as an unloved foster
child in Stockholm, Sweden, to become Mio, son of the King of Farawayland.
ISBN 978-1-59017-870-6 (alk. paper)
[1. Fathers and sons—Fiction. 2. Kings, queens, rulers, etc.—Fiction. 3. Adventure
and adventurers—Fiction.] I. Morgan, Jill, translator. II. Wikland, Ilon, illustrator.
III. Title.
PZ7.L65585Mg 2015
[Fic]—dc23

                          2014037549

ISBN 978-1-59017-870-6
Available as an electronic book; ISBN 978-1-59017-871-3

Cover design by Louise Fili, Ltd.

Printed in the United States of America on acid-free paper.
10 9 8 7 6 5 4 3 2 1

Contents

He Travels by Day and by Night   7

In the Garden of Roses   20

Miramis   31

Do Stars Care if You Play to Them?   41

The Well That Whispers at Night   51

He Rode Through the Forest of Moonbeams   66

The Bewitched Birds   84

In the Dead Forest   95

The Deepest Cave in the Blackest Mountain   111

A Claw of Iron   125

I Never Saw a More Fearsome Sword in My Castle   139

Mio, My Son   158

Mio, My Son

He Travels by Day and by Night

DID YOU LISTEN to the radio on October 15th last year? Did you hear the news about a boy who disappeared? This is what it said:

"Police in Stockholm are searching for a nine-year-old boy missing from his home, at 13 North Street, since 6 P.M. two days ago. Karl Anders Nilsson has light hair and blue eyes. At the time of his disappearance he was wearing brown shorts, a gray sweater, and a small red cap. Anyone with more information on his whereabouts should contact the police."

Yes, so they said. But no one had information on Karl Anders Nilsson. He simply vanished. No one knows what happened to him. No one knows, except me. For I am Karl Anders Nilsson.

I wish that I could get hold of Ben, and at least tell him everything. I used to play with Ben. He lives on North Street too. His real name is Benjamin, but everyone calls him Ben. And of course no one calls me Karl Anders, they just say Andy.

I mean, they used to say Andy. Now that I've disappeared they don't say anything. It was only Aunt Hulda and Uncle Olaf who called me Karl Anders. Well, Uncle Olaf never actually called me anything. He never spoke to me.

I was Aunt Hulda and Uncle Olaf's foster child. I went to live with them when I was a year old. Before that I lived in the Children's Home. Aunt Hulda found me there. She really wanted a girl, but there weren't any she could have. So she took me, though Uncle Olaf and Aunt Hulda don't like boys. At least not when they become eight or nine years old. They thought I made too much noise in the house, and that I brought in too much mud after I came back from playing in Tegnérlunden Park, and that I left my clothes lying around, and that I talked and laughed too loudly. Aunt Hulda always said it was an unlucky day when I came to their house. Uncle Olaf said nothing.... Well, sometimes he did say, "You there, go away! I can't stand the sight of you."

He Travels by Day and by Night

I spent most of my time at Ben's. His papa talked to him all the time and helped him build model airplanes, and drew marks on the kitchen door to see how much Ben had grown, and things like that. Ben was allowed to laugh and talk and to leave his clothes lying around as much as he liked. And his papa still loved him. All the boys were welcome to play in Ben's house. No one was allowed to come home with me, because Aunt Hulda said she wouldn't have children running all around. Uncle Olaf agreed. "We've got as much as we can stand with one troublesome boy," he said.

Sometimes when I went to bed in the evening, I used to wish that Ben's papa was my papa too. And I used to wonder who my real papa was, and why I couldn't live with him and my real mama instead of being in the Children's Home, or having to stay with Aunt Hulda and Uncle Olaf. Aunt Hulda told me that my mama had died when I was born. "No one knows who your father was," she said, "but it's easy enough to guess that he was a bum." I hated Aunt Hulda for what she said about my father. Maybe it was true that my mother died when I was born, but I knew that my father wasn't a bum. Sometimes I lay in bed crying for him.

One person was kind to me, Mrs. Lundy in the fruit shop. She gave me fruit and candy, now and then.

Now, afterwards, I wonder who Mrs. Lundy really was. Because it all started with her on that day in October last year.

That day Aunt Hulda said several times that it was an ill wind which brought me to her house. In the evening, just before before six o'clock, she told me to run down to the bakery on Queens Road to buy some rolls that she liked. I put on my red cap and raced off.

When I passed the fruit shop Mrs. Lundy was standing in the doorway. She touched my chin and looked at me intently for a while. Then she said, "Would you like an apple?"

"Yes, thanks," I said.

She gave me a beautiful red apple that looked awfully good. Then she said, "Will you put a card in the mailbox for me?"

"Yes, I'll be happy to do that," I said. Then she wrote a few lines on a card and handed it to me.

"Good-bye, Karl Anders Nilsson," said Mrs. Lundy. "Good-bye, good-bye, Karl Anders Nilsson."

It sounded so peculiar. She never used to call me anything but Andy.

I hurried to the mailbox a block away. Just as I was going to drop the card in, I noticed that it glistened and glowed like fire. Yes, the words that Mrs. Lundy had written glowed like fire! I couldn't help reading them. This is what the card said:

To the King,
Farawayland.

The one you have long searched for is on his way. He
travels by day and by night, and he carries in his hand
the sign, a beautiful golden apple.

I didn't understand a word of it, but it sent shivers
up and down my spine. I quickly dropped the card in
the mailbox.

Who was traveling by day and by night? Who was carrying a golden apple in his hand?

Then I caught sight of the apple that Mrs. Lundy had given me. And the apple was gold. *It was gold!* In my hand I had a lovely golden apple.

Then I almost began to cry. Not really, but almost. I felt so alone. I went and sat on a bench in Tegnérlunden Park. No one else was there. Everyone had gone home for dinner. It was almost dark among the trees and it rained a little. But in the houses around the park there were lights everywhere. I could see the light from Ben's window, too. He was sitting inside eating pease porridge and pancakes with his mama and papa. It seemed to

me that behind every lighted window children were at home, together with their mamas and papas. Only I sat out here in the darkness. Alone. Alone, holding a golden apple that I didn't know what to do with.

I put it carefully on the bench beside me, while I thought. There was a street light nearby, and the light from it fell on me and on the apple. But the light also fell on something else that was lying on the ground. It was an ordinary bottle, empty of course. Someone had stuffed a piece of wood into the neck of it, probably one of the little children who played in Tegnérlunden Park in the afternoons. I picked up the bottle and read the label. "Stockholm Breweries AB, Pale Ale," it said. As I sat there and read it, I noticed something moving inside the bottle.

I once borrowed a book called *A Thousand and One Nights* from the library in our neighborhood, it was about a genie trapped in a bottle. But, of course, that was far away in Arabia and thousands of years ago, and I don't believe that genie was in an ordinary bottle. It's probably rare for genies to be in bottles from Stockholm Breweries. But here was one, in any case. It was a genie, mark my words, sitting inside the bottle. But he wanted out. He pointed to the wooden peg that blocked the neck of the bottle and looked at me pleadingly. Of course, I wasn't used to genies, so I was almost too scared to pull out the wooden peg. But at last I did, and with a great surge the genie rushed out of the bottle and started to grow very big, so big at last, that he was taller than all the houses around Tegnérlunden Park. That's what genies do, they can shrink so small that they have enough room to fit in a bottle, and in the next blink of an eye they can grow to become as large as a house.

You can't imagine how frightened I was. I trembled from head to foot. Then the genie spoke to me. His voice was a great roar, and I thought at once that Aunt Hulda and Uncle Olaf would hear it; they always thought that I spoke too loud.

"Child," the genie said to me, "you have released me from my prison. Tell me how I may reward you."

But I didn't want a reward for pulling out a little wooden peg. The genie told me that he had come to Stockholm the night before and that he had crept into the bottle to sleep. Because bottles make the best sleeping places that genies know of. But when he slept someone had blocked the way out. And if I hadn't rescued him, maybe he would've stayed in the bottle for a thousand years until the wooden peg had rotted away.

"That would not have pleased my lord the King," said the genie, almost to himself.

Then I gathered my courage and asked, "Genie, where do you come from?"

He was silent a moment. Then he said, "I come from Farawayland."

He said it so loudly that it rang and thundered in my head, and something in his voice made me long for that place. I felt as if I could not live if I didn't get to go there. I raised my arms up toward the genie and shouted, "Take me with you! Oh, take me to Farawayland! Someone is waiting for me there."

The genie shook his head. But then I held the golden apple out toward him and the genie gave a loud cry. "You carry the sign in your hand! You're the one that I've come to bring back. You're the one that the King has been searching for so long!"

He bent down and lifted me up in his arms. Around us were the sound of bells and the roar of thunder as we rose into the air. We left Tegnérlunden Park far below us, the gloomy Park and all the houses where there were lights in the windows and where the children were having dinner with their mamas and papas. Then I, Karl Anders Nilsson, soared up, under the stars.

We were far above the clouds and we traveled faster than lightning and with a roar louder than thunder. Stars and moons and suns sparkled around us. Sometimes it was all as black as night, sometimes so dazzlingly bright and white that I had to shut my eyes.

"He travels by day and by night," I whispered to myself. That's what the card had said.

Suddenly the genie stretched out his arm and pointed

to something far away, something green that was lying in the clear blue water and in bright sunshine.

"There you see Farawayland," said the genie.

We sank down toward the green island.

It was an island swimming in the sea, and in the air was the scent of a thousand roses and lilies and a strange music that was more beautiful than any other music in the world.

Down by the shore stood a huge white palace, and we landed there.

A man came striding along the water's edge. It was *my father the King!* I recognized him as soon as I saw him. I knew that he was my father. He opened his arms and I ran right into them. He held me close for a long time. We didn't say anything to each other. I just held my arms around his neck as tightly as I could.

Oh, how I wished that Aunt Hulda could've seen my father the King, how handsome he was and how his clothes shimmered with gold and diamonds. His face was like the face of Ben's papa, but more handsome. It was a pity Aunt Hulda couldn't see him. Then she would've seen that my papa was not a bum.

But Aunt Hulda was right when she said that my mama died when I was born, and the foolish people at the Children's Home never thought of telling my father the King where I was. He had searched for me for nine long years. I'm so glad that I've come home at last.

I've been here quite long now. Every day is full of fun. Every evening my father the King comes to my room and we build model airplanes and talk to each other.

I'm growing and I'm fine here in Farawayland. My father the King marks the kitchen door each month, to see how much I've grown.

"Mio, my son, how much you've grown again," he says when we measure. "Mio, my son," he says, and it sounds so warm and comforting. It turns out that my real name isn't Andy at all.

"I searched nine long years for you," says my father

the King. "I used to lie awake at night saying to myself, 'Mio, my son.' So I'd know your name well."

That shows you. Calling me Andy was a mistake, like everything else when I lived on North Street. Now it's all been set right.

I love my father the King, and he loves me.

I wish Ben knew about all this. I think I'll write to him and put the letter in a bottle. Then I'll put a cork in the bottle and throw it in the blue sea that surrounds Farawayland. When Ben is with his mama and papa at their summer place in Vaxholm maybe the bottle will come sailing along just when he's swimming. That would be good. I'd like Ben to know about all the remarkable things that have happened to me here. He could call the police too, and tell them that Karl Anders Nilsson, whose real name is Mio, is safe in Farawayland and all is fine, so fine with his father the King.

In the Garden of Roses

I DON'T QUITE know how to explain it to Ben. What's happened to me isn't like anything that's happened to anyone else. I don't know how to explain it so Ben would really understand. I've tried hard to think of a word that would describe it, but there isn't one. Maybe I could write, "Something tremendous has happened to me." But Ben still wouldn't know what it's like here in Farawayland. I'd need to send him at least a dozen bottles to tell him all about my father the King and his Garden of Roses, and about Pompoo and my beautiful white Miramis, and about cruel Sir Kato in Outer Land. No, I could never tell him about everything that has happened to me.

On the very first day, my father the King took me to see his Garden of Roses. It was in the evening, and the wind rustled through the trees. As we walked toward the garden I heard strange music that sounded like a thousand glass bells ringing all at once. The music was faint but very clear, so that I shivered when I heard it.

"Listen to my silver poplars," said my father the King.

He held my hand as we walked. Aunt Hulda and Uncle Olaf never held my hand; no one had ever held my hand before. That's the reason why I loved to walk there holding my father the King's hand, although I was really too old for it.

There was a high wall around the Garden of Roses. My father the King opened a little door, and we went in.

A long time ago, I stayed with Ben at his family's summer place out in Vaxholm, and we sat on some rocks and fished as the sun was going down. The sky was red and the water was so still. It was the time of year when the wild roses were blooming and so many of them were growing close to the rocks. Far away, on the other side of the bay, a cuckoo called loudly. I thought to myself that this was the most beautiful sight in the world. Of course I didn't see the cuckoo because it was so far away, but its cries made everything else seem even prettier. I wasn't foolish enough to tell Ben, but I kept thinking the whole time, silently to myself, "I'm sure this is the prettiest place in the world."

But back then I hadn't seen my father the King's Garden of Roses. I hadn't seen his roses, all of his beautiful, beautiful roses that flowed as if from a stream, or the white lilies swaying in the breeze. I hadn't seen the poplars with the silvery leaves, so tall that stars were twinkling in the treetops when evening came. I hadn't seen the white birds that flew through the Garden of Roses. I hadn't ever heard anything like their songs or the music of the silver poplars. No one could've ever heard or seen anything as beautiful as what I heard and saw in my father the King's Garden of Roses. I stood still and held my father the King's hand. I wanted him there because it was too pretty to look at all alone.

My father the King touched my chin and said, "Mio, my son, what do you think of my Garden of Roses?"

I couldn't answer. I felt so strange, almost as if I was going to cry, and yet I wasn't sad; I felt quite the contrary.

I meant to tell my father the King that he shouldn't think that I was sad. But before I told him anything he spoke. "It's good that you're happy. Keep on feeling that way, Mio, my son."

Then he went to have a talk with his Master Rose Gardener, who was waiting for him. I ran off by myself to explore. It was all so wonderful I felt giddy, as if I were full of lemonade. My legs just wouldn't keep still, and my arms felt very strong. I wished Ben were there so that we could have a fight, only for fun of course. Yes, I wished Ben were there. Because I wanted someone my own age to share all of this with. But poor Ben would be in Tegnérlunden Park right now, and it would be raining and windy as usual, and dark and dreary as well. By now he'd be sure to know that I had disappeared and he'd be wondering where I had gone and whether he would ever see me again. Poor Ben! We had so much fun together, Ben and I, and I began to miss Ben as I was walking in my father the King's Garden of Roses. He was the only old thing I missed from my past. There really wasn't anyone else I missed. Well, maybe Mrs. Lundy because she had always been so kind to me. But most of all I thought about Ben.

I walked quietly for a while along a little winding path in the Garden of Roses and I felt like there wasn't any lemonade left in me, and I was a little sad and hung my head. Then suddenly I looked up, in front of me on the path was…well, at first I thought it was Ben. But it wasn't him. It was Pompoo. Of course, I didn't know he was Pompoo. I saw a boy, and he had exactly the same dark brown hair as Ben and exactly the same brown eyes.

"Who are you?" I asked.

"I'm Pompoo," he said.

Then I saw that he was only a little bit like Ben. He looked more earnest and kind than Ben. Ben is nice too of course, like me—sometimes nice, and sometimes not. We would fight and be angry with each other, but it didn't last long, and we were friends again soon. I can't imagine anyone fighting with Pompoo, though. He was too nice for that.

"Do you want to know my name?" I said. "I'm Andy ...no, that's not true, my name is Mio."

"I already knew your name was Mio," said Pompoo. "Our lord the King sent heralds throughout the land to say that Mio has come home."

Think of it! My father the King was so glad to have found me that he told everyone, near and far. It was probably a little childish of him, but I was pleased to hear it.

"Do you have a father, Pompoo?" I asked. I hoped and wished that he had one, because I'd been without a father for so long and I knew how bad that was.

"Certainly I have a father," said Pompoo. "Our lord

the King's Master Rose Gardener is my father. Would you like to come and see where I live?"

I said I would. He ran ahead of me along the winding path to the farthest corner of the Garden of Roses. There stood a little white cottage with a thatched roof, exactly the kind of cottage you'd find in a fairy tale. There were so many roses growing on the walls and on the roof that I could hardly see anything of the cottage itself. The windows were open wide and white birds flew in and out as they pleased. Outside, under the gable, were a bench and a table. Bees, from the long row of beehives, buzzed among the roses. All around the cottage, roses grew in great thickets, and there were poplars and willow trees with silvery leaves.

A voice called from the kitchen, "Pompoo, have you forgotten dinner?"

The shout was from Pompoo's mother. She came to the door and stood there laughing. I saw that she was exactly like Mrs. Lundy, maybe a little prettier. She had exactly the same kind of dimples in her round cheeks, and she touched my chin just as Mrs. Lundy had when she said, "Good-bye, Karl Anders Nilsson, good-bye."

But Pompoo's mama said, "Good day, good day, Mio! Will you eat dinner with Pompoo?"

"Yes, thank you," I said, "if it's not too much trouble."

She said it wouldn't be any trouble at all. Pompoo and I sat down at the table outside under the gable, and his mama brought out a large dish of pancakes, strawberry preserves and milk. We ate so much, Pompoo and I, that we were ready to burst, we looked at each other and laughed. I was so glad that Pompoo was there. One of the white birds flew over and stole a bit of pancake from my plate. That made us laugh even more.

Then I saw my father the King walking toward us with the Master Rose Gardener, who was Pompoo's father. Suddenly, I felt a little uneasy that my father the

King wouldn't like me sitting there eating and laughing so much. Back then, I still didn't know how good my father the King was, and how much he loved me, whatever I did, and how much he wanted me to laugh.

My father the King stopped when he saw me. "Mio, my son, you're sitting there and laughing," he said.

"Yes, forgive me," I said, because I thought he disliked loud laughter as much as Uncle Olaf and Aunt Hulda did.

"Laugh more!" said my father the King. Then he turned to the Master Rose Gardener and said something even more peculiar, "I enjoy the birds singing. I enjoy the music of the silver poplars. But most of all I love to hear my son laugh in the Garden of Roses."

In the Garden of Roses

I understood then for the first time that I never needed to be afraid of my father the King, that whatever I did he would always look at me kindly, like he was doing now as he stood there with his hand on the Master Rose Gardener's shoulder and with all the white birds flying around him. And when I understood him, I was happier than I'd ever been before in my life. I was so glad that I laughed quite hard. I threw my head back and burst into laughter, nearly scaring the birds away. Pompoo thought I was still laughing at the bird that stole a piece of pancake from me, and he started laughing again, and so did my father the King, and Pompoo's mama and papa too. I don't know what they were laughing at. All I know is that I laughed because it made my father the King happy.

When Pompoo and I had finished eating we raced around the Garden of Roses, turned somersaults on the lawn, and played hide-and-seek among the rose bushes. There were so many hiding places, if there had been one-tenth as many in Tegnérlunden Park, Ben and I would've been thrilled. I mean, *Ben* would've been thrilled. I'll never need to look for hiding places in Tegnérlunden Park again, thank goodness.

It was turning dark. A soft blue mist spread over the Garden of Roses. The white birds grew silent and flew to their nests. The silver poplars became quiet too. The whole Garden of Roses was still. But in the top of the tallest poplar, a great black solitary bird sat singing. It sang more sweetly than all the white birds put together. It felt as if this bird only sang for me. But I didn't want to listen, because its song was so eerie.

"It's getting late," said Pompoo. "I must go home."

"No, don't go," I said, because I didn't want to be left alone listening to that strange song.

"Pompoo, what is that there?" I asked pointing up at the black bird.

"I don't know," said Pompoo. "I've been calling it Sorrowbird just because it's so black. But its real name might be something completely different."

"I don't think I like it," I said.

"*I* do," said Pompoo. "Sorrowbird has such kind eyes. Good night, Mio," he said and ran off.

Then I saw my father the King. He took my hand in his and we walked home through the Garden of Roses. Sorrowbird continued singing, but now that I held my father the King's hand, the song didn't sound so eerie to me. Instead I wished Sorrowbird would sing on and on and on.

The last thing I saw before we walked through the garden door was Sorrowbird lifting his broad black wings and flying straight up into the sky. And I saw that three small stars had begun to shine.

Miramis

I WONDER WHAT Ben would say if he could see my white horse with the golden mane, my Miramis with golden hooves and golden mane.

Ben and I loved horses. Ben and Mrs. Lundy weren't my only friends when I lived on North Street. I had another friend too, I forgot to mention that. His name was Charlie, and he was an old brewer's horse.

Twice a week the brewer's cart brought beer to the shops on North Street, usually early in the morning when I was walking to school and I watched for it so that I could talk a little with Charlie. He was such a

good old horse, and I saved sugar cubes and bread crusts for him. Ben did too, because Ben was also fond of Charlie. He said Charlie was his horse, and I said he was mine, and sometimes we argued about Charlie. But when Ben wasn't listening I whispered in Charlie's ear, "You're my horse!" I think Charlie looked like he understood what I was saying and agreed with me. Ben had his mama and papa and everything, and he didn't need a horse as much as I did, because I was all alone. So I thought it was fair that Charlie was more my horse than Ben's. Of course, the truth is that Charlie wasn't our horse at all but the brewery's. We just pretended he was ours. But I pretended so hard that I almost believed it. Sometimes I talked to Charlie for such a long time that I was late for school, and when the teacher asked why I was late, I knew I couldn't answer. Because you can't tell a teacher that you've only been talking to an old brewer's horse.

On some mornings the cart was running late and I was forced to go to school without seeing Charlie. I was angry with the brewery worker for being slow and I sat on my school bench, feeling the sugar cubes and bread crusts in my pocket, and thought of Charlie. I wanted to see Charlie and knew it would be several days before I got to see him again.

Then the teacher would say, "Why are you acting like this Andy? Why are you sighing? Do you feel bad?"

32

I said nothing. What could I say? The teacher would never understand how much I loved Charlie.

Now Ben has Charlie to himself, I believe, and that is fine. It's fine that Ben has Charlie to console him, now that I've disappeared.

I have my Miramis now, with the golden mane. This is how I got him.

One evening as we were building model airplanes and talking with each other—like Ben and his papa do—I told my father the King about Charlie.

"Mio, my son," said my father the King, "do you like horses?"

"Oh, I suppose," I answered. It probably sounded like I wasn't interested in horses very much, but that was because I didn't want my father the King to believe I missed having one, here with him.

Next morning, when I went into the Garden of Roses, a white horse galloped toward me and I'd never seen a horse gallop like this one. Its golden mane was streaming and its golden hooves glistened in the sunlight. It came straight toward me, neighing more wildly than I've ever heard a horse neigh before. I almost became scared and pressed against my father the King. But my father the King took hold of the golden mane in his strong hands and the horse stood perfectly still and stuck his soft nose down into my pocket to see if there were any sugar cubes. Exactly as Charlie used to do. And I really did have sugar cubes. I had filled my pocket out of habit and the horse ate them all up.

"Mio, my son," said my father the King, "this is your horse, and his name is Miramis."

Oh, my Miramis, I loved him from the first moment. I thought he was the most beautiful horse in the world and not a bit like poor Charlie, who was so old and tired. At least I didn't see any likeness at first, not before Miramis raised his beautiful head and looked at me. Then I saw that he had the same eyes as Charlie. Such faithful, faithful eyes—as horses have.

I'd never ridden at all in my life. But now my father the King lifted me up on Miramis.

"I don't know if I dare," I said.

"Mio, my son," said my father the King. "Don't you have a fearless heart?"

Then I grasped the reins and rode through the Garden of Roses. I rode under the poplars, and they dropped silvery leaves in my hair. I rode faster and faster and faster and Miramis jumped over the tallest rose bushes easily and gracefully. Only once did he brush a hedge, scattering a shower of rose petals.

Then Pompoo came and saw me riding. He clapped his hands and shouted, "Mio is riding on Miramis! Mio is riding on Miramis!"

Pulling on the reins I stopped Miramis, and asked Pompoo if he'd like to ride, and of course he wanted

to. Quickly he climbed up behind me and we rode into the green meadows outside the Garden of Roses. It was the most exciting thing that had ever happened to me.

My father the King's county is vast. Farawayland is the biggest country of all. It stretches north and south, and east and west. The island where my father the King has his palace is Greenfields Island. But it is only a small part of Farawayland. Only a little, little piece.

"The Land on the Other Side of the Water and Beyond the Mountains also belongs to our lord the King," said Pompoo as we rode through the green meadows beyond the Garden of Roses.

I was thinking of Ben while we rode swiftly through the sunshine. Poor Ben, think of him standing in the drizzling rain and darkness there on North Street while I rode around and was so happy on Greenfields Island. It was so pretty. The grass was soft and green, flowers lay everywhere, clear streams flowed down the hills and little woolly white lambs grazed in the grass.

We met a shepherd boy playing on a small wooden flute. He played a strange melody which I thought I'd heard before, but I was certain that I hadn't heard it on North Street.

We stopped and talked to the shepherd boy. His name was Nonno, and I asked if I could borrow his flute for a little while. He said I could, and he taught me to play the melody.

"I can make flutes for both of you, if you'd like," said Nonno.

We said we'd definitely like to have flutes. A stream flowed nearby, and the branches of a willow tree were leaning over the water. Nonno ran and cut a branch from the willow tree. We all sat down and splashed our feet in the water while Nonno carved wooden flutes for us. Pompoo learned to play the strange melody. Nonno told us that it was an old melody which had existed in the world before all the other melodies, and that shepherds had played it out in their pastures for thousands and thousands of years since then.

We thanked him for making flutes for us and for teaching us the old melody. Then we climbed up on Miramis again and rode away. We heard Nonno playing his flute farther and farther and farther away.

"We must be careful with our flutes," I said to Pompoo, "and if we ever become separated, we'll play this old melody."

Pompoo held his arms tightly around me with his head leaning against my back, so he wouldn't fall off the horse. "Yes, Mio," he said, "we must be careful with our flutes, and if you hear my flute playing you'll know that I'm calling you."

"Yes," I said, "and if you hear *me* playing, you'll know that I'm calling you."

"Yes," said Pompoo, and I knew he was my best friend. Except for my father the King, of course. I loved my father the King more than anyone in the world. But Pompoo was a boy like myself, and now he was my best friend since I couldn't see Ben anymore.

Just think, I had my father the King and Pompoo and Miramis, and I was riding over green hills and meadows as fast as the wind. It wasn't strange that I was so happy.

"How do you get to the Land on the Other Side of the Water and Beyond the Mountains?" I asked.

"Over the Bridge of Morninglight," said Pompoo.

"Where is the Bridge of Morninglight?" I said.

"We'll see it soon," said Pompoo. And we did. It was a bridge so high and so long that I couldn't see the end of it. It glittered in the morning sun and seemed to be made of golden rays.

"It's the longest bridge in the world," said Pompoo. "And it goes between Greenfields Island and the Land on the Other Side of the Water. But at night our lord the King draws it up, so that we can sleep calmly on Greenfields Island."

"Why?" I asked. "Who would come at night?"

"Sir Kato," said Pompoo.

The moment he said it I felt an icy wind, and Miramis began trembling.

It was the first time that I'd heard Sir Kato's name. "Sir Kato," I said to myself, and the sound of it made me shiver.

"Yes, the cruel Sir Kato," said Pompoo. Miramis neighed loudly, almost a scream, so we stopped talking about Sir Kato.

I wanted to ride over the Bridge of Morninglight, but first I needed to ask my father the King's permission, so we turned back to the Garden of Roses and didn't ride any more that day. Instead, we groomed Miramis and combed his golden mane and we petted him and fed him sugar cubes and bread crusts that we got from Pompoo's mama.

Later we built a hut in the Garden of Roses,

Pompoo and I, and we sat in it and ate our food. We ate thin pancakes with sugar on them. They were the best I'd ever had. Ben's mama used to make pancakes, and I got to taste them sometimes. But the ones that Pompoo's mama made were even better.

It was such fun building our hut. It's something I've always wanted to do. Ben often told me about the huts he used to build at their summer place out in Vaxholm. I really wish that I could write to him and tell him about our hut, Pompoo's and mine.

"See what a fine hut I've built!" I'd write. "See what a fine hut I've built here in Farawayland."

Do Stars Care if
You Play to Them?

THE NEXT DAY we rode back to Nonno. At first we couldn't find him, but soon we heard the sound of his flute behind a little hill. He sat there playing to himself while the sheep grazed around. When he caught sight of us he took his flute from his mouth and laughed and said, "You've come again!"

He seemed glad that we had come back. We took out our flutes and played, all three of us. The songs were so pretty, I didn't understand how we could play such lovely melodies.

"It's a shame there's no one to hear how fine we play," I said.

"The grass hears us," said Nonno. "And the flowers and wind. The trees hear how we play, the willow trees that lean over the stream."

"Do they?" I said. "Do they like it?"

"Yes, they love it," said Nonno.

We played a long time for the grass and flowers and wind and trees. But I still thought it was a shame there weren't any people to hear us.

Then Nonno said, "We can go home and play for my grandmother if you want to. My grandmother that I live with."

"Does she live far from here?" I asked.

"Yes, but the way will seem short, if we play as we walk," said Nonno.

"Yes, yes, the way won't be long, if we play as we walk," said Pompoo. He wanted to walk home to see Nonno's grandmother as much as I did.

In fairy tales there are always kind old grandmothers. But I'd never met a real grandmother, though I know there are many. That's why I thought it would be so fun to go and meet Nonno's grandmother.

We had to take all Nonno's lambs and sheep with us. And Miramis. We were a whole caravan. First went Pompoo and Nonno and I, then came the sheep and lambs and at the end rambled Miramis. Practically as slow as Charlie. We walked over hills and played as we went along. The lambs probably wondered where we were taking them. But I think they enjoyed it, because they bleated and skipped around us the whole time.

When we had walked for many hours and over many hills, we came to Nonno's house. It was the kind of house in fairy tales, too, a funny little cottage with a thatched roof and lots of lilacs and jasmine outside.

"Be quiet now, so we can surprise Grandmother," said Nonno.

A window stood open and we could hear someone bustling about inside. We lined up by the window, Nonno and Pompoo and I.

"Let's start," said Nonno. "One, two, three!"

And we did. We played such a merry tune that the lambs skipped and danced when they heard it. An old, old woman came to the window; she looked very kind. She was Nonno's grandmother and she clapped her hands and said, "Oh, what beautiful music!"

We played to her for a long time and she remained by the window listening until we were done. She was very old and looked like a character out of a fairy tale, though she was a real grandmother.

After that we went into the cottage. Nonno's grandmother asked us if we were hungry, and we were. So she brought out a loaf of bread and cut thick slices from it which she gave us. It was crisp brown bread, and it was the best bread I've ever eaten in my life.

"Oh, it tastes good," I said to Nonno. "What kind of bread is it?"

"I don't think it's any special kind of bread," said Nonno. "We call it the Bread That Satisfies Hunger."

Miramis wanted to eat with us, too. He came and stuck his head through the open window and neighed a little. We laughed at him because he looked so funny. But Nonno's grandmother stroked his nose and gave him some of the good bread too.

Do Stars Care if You Play to Them?

After that I was thirsty and when I told Nonno, he said, "Follow me."

He took us into the garden, and there was a clear well. Nonno lowered a wooden pail down into the well and brought up some water and we drank out of the wooden pail. It was the coolest and best water I've ever tasted in my life.

"Oh, that's very good," I said to Nonno. "What kind of well is it?"

"It's not any special kind of well," said Nonno. "We call it the Well That Quenches Thirst."

Miramis was thirsty, and the lambs and sheep too, so we gave them water to drink.

Soon it was time for Nonno to walk back to the pastures among the hills, with his sheep. He asked his grandmother for the cloak he would use to wrap up in while sleeping out in the pastures at night, watching over his sheep. She brought out a brown cloak and gave it to him. I thought Nonno was very lucky to be able to sleep in the pastures. It was something I'd never done before. Sometimes Ben and his mama and papa used to ride their bikes out to a campground. They would pitch their tent on a pleasant wooded hillside and sleep in their sleeping bags at night. Ben always said it was the best time, and I believe it.

"I wish I could sleep outside all night," I said to Nonno.

"You can," said Nonno. "Follow me!"

"No," I said. "My father the King would be worried if I didn't come home."

"I can take a message to our lord King that you'll be sleeping out in the pastures tonight," said Nonno's grandmother.

"And to my father, too," said Pompoo.

"To the Master Rose Gardener, too," agreed Nonno's grandmother.

Pompoo and I were so thrilled that we skipped and jumped even more than the lambs.

But Nonno's grandmother looked at our short white jerseys, which were all we had to wear, and she said, "When the dew begins to fall you'll be cold." She suddenly looked very sad. "I have two more cloaks," she said in a quiet little voice.

She went over to an old chest which was standing in a corner of the cottage and took out two cloaks, a red one and a blue.

"My brothers' cloaks," said Nonno, looking so sad, too.

"Where are your brothers?" I asked.

"Sir Kato," whispered Nonno. "The cruel Sir Kato seized them."

When he said this, Miramis neighed outside as if someone had whipped him. All the lambs ran anxiously to their mothers, and all the sheep bleated as if their last hour had come.

48

Nonno's grandmother gave me the red cloak and Pompoo the blue, and she gave Nonno a loaf of the Bread That Satisfies Hunger and a pitcher of water from the Well That Quenches Thirst. And so we walked back over the hills the same way we had come.

It made me sad to think of Nonno's brothers, but I couldn't help feeling happy since I was allowed to sleep out in the pasture.

When we came to the hill by the willow tree that leaned over the stream, we stopped and Nonno said we should camp there for the night.

And we did. We lit a fire—a big, warm glorious fire. We sat around it and ate the Bread That Satisfies Hunger and drank the water from the Well That Quenches Thirst. The dew fell and darkness came, but it didn't matter, because by the fire it was light and warm.

We wrapped our cloaks around us and lay down close to the fire and around about us slept all the sheep and lambs, and Miramis grazed nearby. We lay there, listening to the wind whistling through the grass, and saw the light from the fires far away. Many, many fires were lit tonight because so many shepherds lived on Greenfields Island. We heard them playing in the darkness, the old melody that Nonno said shepherds had been playing for thousands and thousands of years. Yes, we lay watching the fires and listening to the old melody played by a shepherd we didn't know, but who played for us through the night. And it was as if the melody wanted something particular from me.

The sky twinkled with stars, the biggest and brightest stars I've ever seen. I lay there and looked at them. I turned on my back, lying there so warm in my red cloak and I watched them. Then I remembered how we had played for the grass and flowers and wind and trees, and Nonno had said they liked it. But we hadn't played for the stars. "Do stars care if you play to them?" I wondered just that. I asked Nonno and he said he believed they did. So we sat around the fire, took out our flutes, and played a little song for the stars.

The Well That
Whispers at Night

I'D NEVER SEEN the Land on the Other Side of the
Water and Beyond the Mountains. But one day when
I walked with my father the King through the Garden
of Roses, I asked him if I could ride over the Bridge
of Morninglight. My father the King stopped in his
tracks, and took my face in his hands. He looked at me
so kindly, yet so solemnly.

"Mio, my son," he said. "You may travel wherever
you like in my country. You may play on Greenfields
Island or ride to the Land on the Other Side of the
Water and Beyond the Mountains whenever you want
to. You may travel east and west and north and south,
as far as Miramis will carry you. But there is one thing
that you must know. There is a country called Outer
Land."

"Who lives there?" I asked.

"Sir Kato," said my father the King, and his face
darkened. "The cruel Sir Kato."

As he said that name, it seemed like something vile and treacherous had entered the Garden of Roses. The white birds flew to their nests. Sorrowbird screeched loudly and beat his broad black wings. And at that moment many roses withered and died.

"Mio, my son," said my father the King. "You're dearer to me than anything, and my heart grows heavy when I think of Sir Kato."

The wind rushed through the silver poplars as if a storm had passed through them. Countless leaves dropped to the ground, and they seemed to cry as they fell. I felt scared of Sir Kato. So scared, so scared.

"If your heart grows heavy, you must not think of him anymore," I said.

My father the King nodded and took my hand.

"You're right," he said. "For a little while I'll forget Sir Kato. For a little while you can play the flute and build huts in the Garden of Roses."

Then we went to find Pompoo.

My father the King had much to attend to in his great country, but he always had time for me. He never said, "Go away, I don't have time now!" He liked being with me. Every morning he walked with me in the Garden of Roses. He showed me where the birds were nesting, and looked at our hut, and taught me the right way to ride on Miramis, and talked with me and Pompoo about everything. That's just what I liked so much about him—that he talked with Pompoo too. Exactly as Ben's papa used to do with me. I enjoyed it, when Ben's papa talked to me and Ben always looked so pleased then, as if he were thinking, "He's my father but I like him talking to you, too." And that's just how I felt, when my father the King talked with Pompoo.

It was probably a good thing that Pompoo and I went out for long rides, because how else could my father the King govern his vast county? If we hadn't been away, sometimes for whole days on end, then my father the King would have kept on playing and talking with me instead of looking after his country. So it was probably a good thing that I had Pompoo, and Miramis, too.

Oh, my Miramis, what rides I took on his back! My Miramis, who carried me over the Bridge of Morning-light for the first time, I'll never forget it.

It was early in the morning when the guards lowered the bridge for the day. The soft grass was wet with dew, which soaked Miramis's golden hooves, but it didn't matter. We were a little sleepy, Pompoo and I, because we had gotten up so early. But the air was cool and fresh and felt so pleasant against our faces. As we rode across the meadows we became wide awake. We reached the Bridge of Morninglight just as the sun was coming up. We rode out on the bridge, and we felt like we were riding on golden rays of light. The bridge went high, high up over the water. Looking down made me feel dizzy. We were riding on the tallest and longest bridge in the world. Miramis's golden mane glistened in the sun. Faster, faster, faster he ran. Higher and higher and higher up we moved along the bridge. Miramis's hooves thundered. It was glorious and soon I would see the Land on the Other Side of the Water. Soon, soon.

"Pompoo," I shouted, "Pompoo, aren't you glad, isn't this glorious...."

Then I saw what was going to happen. Something terrible was going to happen. Miramis was galloping straight toward an abyss. The bridge ended. It ended in mid-air because the guards hadn't lowered it properly. The bridge didn't reach the Land on the Other Side of the Water. There was a horrible gap where the bridge should have been, an awful depth. I've never been so scared before. I wanted to scream to Pompoo, but I couldn't. I pulled on Miramis's reins to stop him, but he didn't obey me. He neighed wildly and galloped on with thundering hooves to certain death, straight toward the abyss. I was so scared! Soon we would plunge down into the abyss. Soon I would no longer hear the sound of Miramis's hooves, but only his cries as he tumbled down into the depths with his golden mane streaming around him. I shut my eyes and thought of my father the King, while Miramis's hooves thundered on.

Suddenly the thundering stopped. I could still hear the sound of hooves, but it was a different sound, a

thudding like Miramis was galloping on something soft. I opened my eyes and looked, then I saw that Miramis was galloping on *air*. Oh, my Miramis with the golden mane, he moved through the air as easily as he did on land! He could gallop over the clouds and jump over the stars if he wanted to. I'm sure no one ever had such a horse as mine. You can't imagine how it felt sitting on his back, flying through the air, and looking down at the Land on the Other Side of the Water, far below in the sunshine.

"Pompoo," I shouted, "Pompoo, Miramis can gallop over the clouds!"

"Didn't you know that?" he answered, as if there was nothing strange about what Miramis could do.

"No, how could I know?" I said.

Pompoo laughed and said, "There's a lot you don't know, Mio."

We rode around up in the sky for a long time while Miramis jumped over the little white clouds. It was incredibly exciting and enjoyable, but at last we wanted to land. Miramis descended slowly to the ground and stopped. We had arrived at the Land on the Other Side of the Water.

"Here's a green meadow for Miramis with the golden mane," said Pompoo. "Let him graze here while we go and see Totty."

"Who's Totty?" I asked.

"You'll see," said Pompoo. "Totty and his sisters and brothers live near here."

He took my hand and led me nearby to a white cottage with a thatched roof. It was exactly like a cottage from a fairy tale, too. It's hard to explain why a house looks like it comes straight out of a fairy tale. Maybe it's something in the air, or the old trees standing around it, or the fairylike scent of flowers in the garden, or perhaps something entirely different. In the front garden of the cottage was an old round well. I think it was the well that made Totty's house look like it came from a fairy tale, because there aren't many wells like that nowadays, at least I'd never seen one before.

Five children sat around the well. The oldest was a boy. His smile went from ear to ear, and he looked so friendly.

"I saw you coming," he said. "That's a fine horse you have."

"His name is Miramis," I said, "and this is Pompoo and I'm Mio."

"I know," said the boy. "My name is Totty and these are my sisters and brothers."

The whole time he looked so nice and friendly and so did his sisters and brothers, as if they were pleased to see us.

It was so different from North Street. There the boys snarled like wolves when you came near, unless they liked you. They were always mean to someone, and that person was left out of their games. Usually that was me. Only Ben would always play with me. There was a big boy named Johnny. I never did anything to him, but whenever he saw me he shouted, "Leave, before you get a beating. Go away!" It wasn't any good for me to try playing ball or anything with them, because the others were always on Johnny's side and copied him because Johnny was so strong.

Since I was used to Johnny, it was a surprise to meet children like Totty and Pompoo and Nonno and

Totty's sisters and brothers, who were friendly all the time.

Pompoo and I sat down on the edge of the well beside Totty. I looked down into it, and it was so deep that I couldn't see the bottom.

"How do you bring the water up?" I asked.

"We don't bring up any water," said Totty. "It's not a water well."

"What kind of well is it, then?" I said.

"It's called the Well That Whispers at Night," said Totty.

"Why is that?" I asked.

"Wait until tonight, then you'll understand," said Totty.

We stayed with Totty and his sisters and brothers all day long playing under the old trees. When we

were hungry Totty's sister, Minonna-Nell, ran into the kitchen for bread. It was the Bread That Satisfies Hunger and I loved it as much as before.

I found a little spoon in the grass under the trees, a little silver spoon. I showed it to Totty, and he looked very sad.

"That was my sister's spoon," he said. "Mio has found our sister's spoon," he shouted to his sisters and brothers.

"Where's you sister?" I asked.

"Sir Kato," said Totty. "The cruel Sir Kato seized her."

When he said that name the air all around us turned as cold as ice. A tall sunflower in the garden withered and died, and the butterflies lost their wings so that they could never fly again. I felt scared of Sir Kato. So scared, so scared.

I gave the little silver spoon to Totty, but he said, "Keep our sister's spoon. You found it, and she'll never need it again."

His little sisters and brothers cried when they heard that their sister wouldn't need the spoon any more. But soon we started playing again and thought no more of their troubles. I put the spoon in my pocket and thought no more of it either.

But the whole time we were playing, I kept wishing it would be evening, so I could find out more about the peculiar well.

The day went by and it began to get dark. Then Totty looked at his sisters and brothers. They looked at each other wonderingly, and Totty said, "Now!"

They all rushed over and sat down on the edge of the well. Pompoo and I sat down beside them.

"Be perfectly quiet," said Totty.

We sat perfectly quiet and waited. It became a little darker among the trees and Totty's house looked even more like a cottage from a fairy tale. It stood in a strange, mysterious darkness, yet not in total darkness because dusk was only approaching. Something strange and mysterious and very old settled over the cottage and over the trees and, most of all, over the well, as we were sitting around the edge.

"Be *perfectly* quiet," whispered Totty, although we hadn't said a word in a long time. We sat quietly even longer, and it became a little darker among the trees, and I still couldn't hear anything.

But then I heard something. Yes, I heard something. I heard a whisper down in the well! A whisper began deep, deep down in the well. It was such a strange voice, unlike any other voice. *It whispered fairy tales.* They weren't like any other fairy tales, and they were the most beautiful stories in the whole world. There was almost nothing that I loved more than listening to fairy tales, so I lay down flat on my stomach, leaning over the edge of the well to hear more and more of the voice that whispered. Sometimes it sang too, the strangest and most beautiful songs.

"What strange kind of well is this?" I said to Totty.

"A well full of fairy tales and songs. That's all I know," said Totty. "A well full of old stories and songs that have existed in the world for a long time, but that people forgot a long time ago. It is only the Well That Whispers at Night that remembers them all."

I don't know how long we sat there. It got darker among the trees, and the voice from the well became fainter and fainter. At last we heard it no more.

Away in the green pastures I heard Miramis neighing. He probably wanted to remind me that I needed to hurry home to my father the King.

"Good-bye, Totty. Good-bye, Minonna-Nell. Good-bye, everyone," I said.

"Good-bye, Mio. Good-bye, Pompoo," said Totty. "Come back soon!"

"Yes, we'll come again soon," I promised.

We called Miramis and climbed up on his back, and he set off for home at a full gallop. It wasn't so dark now. The moon had risen up in the sky and shone over all the green pastures and over all the silent trees, which looked silver now, exactly like the poplars at home in my father the King's Garden of Roses.

We came to the Bridge of Morninglight, but I hardly recognized it. It looked quite different, as if it were made of silver rays.

"It has another name at night," said Pompoo as we rode up onto the bridge.

"What is it called at night?" I asked.

"The Bridge of Moonlight," he answered.

The Well That Whispers at Night

We rode over the Bridge of Moonlight that would soon be drawn up by the guards and far away we saw the shepherds' fires on Greenfields Island which looked like small lamps. The whole world was completely, completely silent and the only sound was the thunder of hooves against the bridge. Miramis almost looked like a phantom horse in the moonlight and his mane was no longer a golden mane but a silver mane.

I thought about the Well That Whispers at Night and of all the stories I had heard. There was a special one I liked. It started like this: "Once upon a time there was a king's son riding in the moonlight...."

Just imagine, that could've been me! After all, I was a King's son.

We came closer and closer to Greenfields Island, and Miramis's hooves thundered on. The whole time I thought of the fairy tale and how beautiful it was: "Once upon a time there was a king's son riding in the moonlight...."

He Rode Through the Forest of Moonbeams

WHEN I LIVED with Uncle Olaf and Aunt Hulda I used to borrow books of fairy tales from the library. Aunt Hulda didn't like it much.

"You've got your nose in a book again," she'd say. "That's why you're small and pitiful and frail—because you won't go out with the other children."

Of course I went out—I was almost always out. Aunt Hulda and Uncle Olaf preferred that I would never come in. Surely they're glad now, I think. Now that I'll never come in any more.

It was only in the evening that I tried to read a little, and that couldn't be the reason I was so frail. Aunt Hulda should see how big and strong and healthy I am now. I could beat Johnny with one hand tied behind my back if I were back home now on North Street. But I wouldn't do that, because I don't want to.

I wonder what Aunt Hulda would say if she heard about the Well That Whispers at Night. If she found out that you don't have to sit with your nose in a book to read fairy tales, but that you can stay out in the fresh air and still hear as many stories as you want. Maybe Aunt Hulda would think it was fine, even though she was never satisfied with anything.

Yes, if she only knew that in Farawayland there's a well that whispers fairy tales.

"Once upon a time there was a king's son riding in the moonlight. He rode through the Forest of Moonbeams...."

That's what the well had said. I couldn't stop thinking about it. It seemed as if the well had meant something special by that story. That I was the king's son who had once ridden through the Forest of Moonbeams, and that I must do it again. The well had spoken and sung to me for the whole evening just to remind me of what I must do.

I asked my father the King if he knew where the Forest of Moonbeams was.

"The Forest of Moonbeams is in the Land Beyond the Mountains," he said, and his voice sounded melancholy. "Why do you want to know, Mio, my son?"

"Tonight I want to ride there when the moon is shining," I said.

My father the King looked at me intently. "Oh, so soon?" he sighed, and his voice sounded even more melancholy.

"Maybe you don't want me to," I said. "Maybe you'll be worried that I'm out riding in the Forest of the Moonbeams at night."

My father the King shook his head. "No, why should I be?" he said. "A forest sleeping peacefully in the moonlight isn't dangerous."

He sat silently after that, with his head in his hands and I could see he was unhappy. I went to him and put my arms around his shoulders to comfort him and said, "Do you want me to stay home with you?"

He looked at me for a long time with sad eyes.

"No, Mio, my son, you shouldn't stay. The moon has risen, and the Forest of Moonbeams awaits you."

"Are you sure you won't be worried?" I asked.

"Yes, I'm sure," he said, touching me gently on the head. Then I ran to ask Pompoo if he wanted to come with me to the Forest of Moonbeams. But after I'd taken a few steps, my father the King shouted to me, "Mio, my son!"

I turned around and there he stood with his arms stretched out toward me and I rushed back to him and threw myself into his arms. He held me tightly, tightly for a long time.

"I'll come right back," I said.

"Will you?" said my father the King, and his voice wasn't much more than a whisper.

I found Pompoo outside the Master Rose Gardener's

cottage and told him I was going to ride through the Forest of Moonbeams.

"Oh, at last!" said Pompoo.

I didn't understand why my father the King said, "Oh, so soon?" and Pompoo, "Oh, at last!" when I told them I wanted to ride through the Forest of Moonbeams, but I didn't worry about it.

"Are you coming?" I asked.

Pompoo took a deep breath. "Yes," he said. "Yes, yes!"

We called Miramis, who was grazing in the Garden of Roses, and I told him that he must take us to the Forest of Moonbeams. Miramis started prancing as if it was the best thing he'd heard in a long time, and as soon as Pompoo and I sat on his back he shot off like a streak of lightning.

As we rode out of the Garden of Roses I heard my father the King shout. "Mio, my son!" he cried, and it was the saddest voice I'd ever heard. But I couldn't turn back. I couldn't.

The Land Beyond the Mountains was so far away. Without a horse like Miramis we couldn't have gone there. We could never have climbed over the high mountains that nearly reached the sky. But for Miramis there was nothing to it. He soared over the mountain-tops like a bird. I let him land on the highest summit, where the snow never melts. We sat there on Miramis's back and looked out over the land that awaited us at the foot of the mountains. The Forest of Moonbeams lay in front of us in the moonlight and it looked so beautiful and not dangerous at all. It's probably true that a forest sleeping in the moonlight wasn't dangerous. My father the King was right. Everything was good here, not only the people. The forest and fields and streams and green pastures were good too, and not dangerous. The night was good and kind like the day, the moonlight was like a gentle sun, and the darkness was a peaceful darkness. They were nothing to be scared of.

There was only one thing to be scared of. Only one.

As we sat on Miramis's back, far beyond the Forest of Moonbeams I saw a country where it was completely dark, and the darkness wasn't peaceful. I couldn't look at it without shuddering.

"What's that terrible land over there?" I said to Pompoo.

"Outer Land starts there," said Pompoo. "It's the border country of Outer Land."

"Sir Kato's land?" I asked.

When he heard this Miramis trembled with fright, and a large boulder broke loose from the mountain and rumbled down into the valley below.

Yes, there was only one danger—Sir Kato. He was the one I was scared of. So scared, so scared. But I tried not to think about him any more.

"The Forest of Moonbeams," I said to Pompoo.

"The Forest of Moonbeams is where I want to go now."

Miramis neighed and it echoed wildly between the mountaintops. He dropped slowly down through the air toward the moonlit forest at the foot of the mountain. From the forest came an answer to Miramis's call, like a hundred horses neighing in the darkness.

We went lower and lower until Miramis's hooves touched the treetops...so softly, so softly we sank down between the leafy, green branches. And so we arrived in the Forest of Moonbeams.

I haven't been in many forests in my day, but there can't be another one like this. The Forest of Moonbeams had a secret. I felt there was a great and important secret there, but the moon had thrown a mist over the forest, so that I wouldn't know where it was. Not yet. The mist swirled through the trees, whispering the secret, but I couldn't understand it. The trees stood so still and shimmered in the moonlight and they knew the secret, but I didn't.

Suddenly in the distance we heard thundering hooves. It sounded as if a hundred horses galloped through the night, and when Miramis neighed, it sounded like a hundred horses neighing in reply. The thundering hooves came closer and closer, the neighing grew louder and louder, and then they were all around us—a hundred white horses with flowing manes. Miramis galloped right into the herd and they ran off together through an

open field in the forest. Pompoo and I jumped off and stood under a tree and we saw all the white horses, with Miramis in the lead, rushing wildly here and there in the moonlight.

"They're so excited," said Pompoo.

"Why are they excited?" I asked.

"Because Miramis has come home," said Pompoo. "Didn't you know that Miramis used to live in the Forest of Moonbeams?"

"No, I didn't know that," I said.

"There's a lot you don't know, Mio," said Pompoo.

"How did I come to have Miramis?" I asked.

"Our lord the King sent a message that one of his white colts should come to Greenfields Island to be your horse."

I watched Miramis galloping in the moonlight and was very happy and then I became concerned.

"Pompoo, do you think Miramis is sad staying with me?" I asked. "Maybe he's homesick for the Forest of Moonbeams."

When I said that, Miramis came running up to me. He placed his head on my shoulder and stood still for awhile, neighing softly.

"There you see, he loves being with you," said Pompoo.

I was so glad. I petted Miramis and gave him a lump of sugar. His nose felt so very soft against my hand when he took it.

We rode farther through the forest, and the hundred white horses followed us. I felt the secret in the air. The whole forest knew it, every tree, all the green lindens and aspens that rustled so gently over our heads as we rode. The white horses knew it, and so did the birds

that were woken by the trampling hooves. Everything knew it except me. Pompoo was probably right when he said, "There's a lot you don't know, Mio."

I set off at a gallop through the trees, and the white horses galloped with us. We rode very fast. My red cloak caught in the branch of a tree. Maybe the tree didn't want to let me go, maybe it wanted to tell me the secret. But I was in such a hurry. I galloped on and a large gash was torn in my cloak.

In the middle of the forest we came to a cottage, just like in a fairy tale, a little white cottage with a thatched roof. Pretty apple trees grew around it, the white apple blossoms glistening in the moonlight. A window stood open and I heard a pounding noise inside. It sounded like someone weaving.

"Should we see who is weaving?" I said to Pompoo.

"Yes, let's do that," he said.

We jumped off Miramis and followed the path between the apple trees to the cottage. We knocked on the door and the pounding stopped.

"Come in boys," said a voice. "I've been expecting you for a long time."

We went into the cottage and there sat a Weaver working at her loom. She looked so kind and she nodded at us.

"Why do you stay up at night and do your weaving?" I asked.

"I weave the cloth of dreams," she said. "It must be done at night."

The moonlight shone through the window and fell on her cloth and it shimmered beautifully. I've never seen such beautiful fabric.

"Fairy cloth and dream cloth must be woven at night," she said.

"What do you weave with to make it so pretty?" I asked.

She didn't answer, but started weaving again. She pounded the loom and hummed quietly to herself,

"Moonlight, moonlight and heart's red blood,
so silver, silver and purple,
and apple blossoms, to weave the cloth
so smooth and soft.
Softer than the evening wind
through the grass,
as Sorrowbird sings over the forest."

She sang with a quiet, toneless voice, which didn't sound so pretty. When she stopped, I heard another song outside in the forest, one that I'd heard before. What the Weaver had said was right—Sorrowbird sang over the forest. He sat in the top of a tree, singing so sadly that it hurt when you listened to it.

"Why is Sorrowbird singing?" I asked the Weaver.

She began to cry, and her tears fell on the cloth becoming bright little pearls, so that the fabric was even prettier than before.

"Why is Sorrowbird singing?" I asked again.

"He is singing about my little daughter," said the Weaver, crying more bitterly. "He is singing about my little daughter who was stolen."

"Who has stolen your little daughter?" I asked. But I already knew without being told. "Don't say his name," I begged.

"I won't," replied the Weaver, "because the moonlight will die down and the white colts will cry tears of blood."

"Why will they cry blood?" I asked.

"For the little foal that was stolen, too," said the Weaver. "Hear how Sorrowbird sings over the forest!"

I stood there in the middle of the floor in the cottage and listened through the open window, as Sorrowbird sang outside. He had sung to me for many nights in the Garden of Roses, but I hadn't understood what he was singing about. Now I knew. He sang about all the stolen ones, of the Weaver's little daughter, of Nonno's brothers and Totty's sister and many, many others whom the cruel Sir Kato had captured and taken to his castle.

This was why people mourned in the little cottages on Greenfields Island and in the Land on the Other Side of the Water and Beyond the Mountains. They mourned for their children, for all the children who were gone. Even the white horses in the Forest of Moonbeams had one they mourned, and they cried tears of blood if they heard the thief's name.

Sir Kato! I was so scared of him. So scared, so scared! But as I stood there in the cottage, listening to Sorrowbird, something strange occurred to me. Suddenly I knew why I had ridden through the Forest of Moonbeams tonight. Beyond the forest the border country to Outer Land began. It was there that I actually must go. I must go there to fight Sir Kato, though I was so scared, so scared. Yes, I wanted to cry when I realized what I must do.

The Weaver had gone back to her weaving. She hummed the dull tune to herself about "Moonlight, moonlight, heart's red blood" and she didn't pay any more attention to Pompoo and me.

"Pompoo," I said, and my voice sounded rather strange. "Pompoo, I'm going to Outer Land now."

"I know that," said Pompoo.

I was so astonished. "How could you know? I just realized it right now."

"There's a lot you don't know, Mio," said Pompoo.

"But you…you know everything," I said.

"Yes, I do," said Pompoo. "For a long time I've known that you would go to Outer Land. Everyone knows."

"Everyone knows?"

"Yes," said Pompoo. "Sorrowbird knows it. The Weaver knows it. The hundred white horses know it. The entire Forest of Moonbeams knows it, the trees whisper it, and the grass and the apple blossoms outside, they all know it."

"Do they?" I said.

"All the shepherds on Greenfields Island know it and play of it on their flutes at night. Nonno knows it. His grandmother and Totty and his sisters and brothers know it. The Well That Whispers at Night knows it. I tell you, they all know it."

"And my father the King...?" I whispered.

"Your father the King has always known it," said Pompoo.

"Does he want me to go?" I asked, and I couldn't help the little quaver in my voice.

"Yes, he wants it," said Pompoo. "He mourns, but he wants you to go."

"Yes, but I'm so scared," I said and I began to cry. Now, for the first time, I realized just how scared I was. I took Pompoo's arm.

"Pompoo, I can't," I said. "Why does my father the King want me to do it?"

"A boy of royal blood is the only person who can," said Pompoo. "Only a boy of royal blood can do it."

"But what if I die?" I said, gripping Pompoo's arm. He didn't answer.

"Does my father the King want me to go, no matter what happens?"

The Weaver had finished weaving and the cottage was silent. Sorrowbird was silent. The trees didn't rustle their leaves. Not a sound was heard. Silence was everywhere.

Pompoo nodded.

"Yes," he said, faintly so that I scarcely heard it. "Your father the King wants you to go, no matter what happens."

I was heartbroken. "I can't," I cried. "I can't! I can't!"

Pompoo said nothing. He only looked at me without saying a word. But Sorrowbird began singing again, a song that almost stopped my heart from beating.

"He is singing about my little daughter," said the Weaver and her tears fell over the cloth and turned into pearls.

I clenched my hands. "Pompoo," I said, "I'm going at once. I'm going to Outer Land."

A sigh passed through the Forest of Moonbeams and from Sorrowbird came a song that had never been heard in any forest in the world.

"I know that," said Pompoo.

"Good-bye, Pompoo," I said as I nearly began to cry. "Good-bye, dear Pompoo."

He looked at me, and his eyes were so kind and just like Ben's. Then he smiled a little.

"I'm coming with you," he said.

Pompoo was my friend, he was a true friend. I was so glad, when he said that he wanted to come with me. But I didn't want him to run into danger.

"No, Pompoo," I said. "You can't come with me now, where I'm going."

"I am coming," said Pompoo. "A boy of royal blood riding on a white horse with golden mane, and accompanied by his best friend—it's been foretold. You can't change what has been foretold for thousands and thousands of years."

"For thousands and thousands of years," repeated the Weaver. "I remember the wind singing of it the night I planted my apple trees, and much time has passed. Thousands and thousands of years." She nodded her head. "Come, Mio, I'll fix your cloak," she said.

She cut the cloth from her loom and took a piece of it and fixed the tear in my cloak, which happened when I had been riding through the forest. Yes, she lined my cloak too, with the shimmering cloth, and it hung lightly, soft and warm, over my shoulders.

"I give my finest cloth to the one who will save my little daughter," said the Weaver. "And you shall have bread, the Bread That Satisfies Hunger. Eat it sparingly! For you will travel on the path of hunger."

She gave me the bread and I thanked her. Then I turned to Pompoo.

"Are we ready, Pompoo?"

"Yes, we're ready," said Pompoo.

We went out through the door. We followed the path between the apple trees. We mounted our horse. Then Sorrowbird spread his black wings and flew up toward the mountains.

The hundred white horses stood still, watching us, as we rode away through the trees. They didn't follow us. The apple blossoms glittered like snow in the moonlight. They glittered like snow.... Maybe I would never see such pretty white apple blossoms again.

The Bewitched Birds

MAYBE I NEVER will see apple blossoms and rustling green trees and soft grass again. Because now we were traveling to a country where there were no flowers, and no trees or grass could grow.

We rode through the night. We rode and rode. Soon the friendly Forest of Moonbeams was gone; we had left it behind. And in front of us was darkness. The moonlight faded, the ground was rocky and hard, barren walls of rock rose on every side. They pressed in closer and closer on us. At last we rode along a dark narrow path, deep down between two tall black mountains.

"If only it weren't so dark," said Pompoo. "If only the mountains weren't so dark and we weren't so small and all alone."

The path twisted and curved, and danger seemed to lurk at every turn. Miramis felt it too. His whole body trembled and he wanted to turn back. But I held the reins firmly and forced him on. The path narrowed. The dark mountains rose higher. The darkness thickened.

At last we came to something that looked like a door, a narrow opening between the rocks. Behind it was a darkness blacker than any other darkness in the world.

"Outer Land," whispered Pompoo. "It's the entrance to Outer Land."

Miramis reared wildly. He rose up on his hind legs and neighed so that I couldn't stand to hear it. It sounded terrible, and it was the only sound we could hear, because the darkness beyond the door was silent. It was silent and it seemed to watch us. It was just waiting for us to cross the border.

I knew that I must go into the darkness. And yet I wasn't scared any more. Now that I knew it had been foretold for thousands and thousands of years that I was to pass through this dark doorway, I felt braver. I knew that no matter what happened, I was going. Maybe I would never return, but I made up my mind not to be scared.

I drove Miramis into the darkness. When he saw that I wouldn't let him turn back, he set off at a full gallop through the narrow doorway and along the dark road beyond it. We rushed through the darkness, around us all was black, and we didn't know the way.

But Pompoo was with me. He sat behind me and held on tightly and I loved him more than ever. I was not alone. I had a friend with me, my best friend, exactly as it was foretold.

I don't know how long we galloped through the darkness. Maybe it was only a short time, maybe it was many, many hours. Or maybe it was thousands and thousand of years, that's how it seemed. It was like riding in a dream—one of those horrible dreams that you wake up from with a scream and leaves you scared for a long time afterward. But this wasn't a dream I could wake up from. We rode and rode. We didn't know where we were going. We didn't know how far. We just rode on through the night.

At last Miramis stopped with a jerk. We had come to a lake. The lake was more terrifying than anything in a dream. In my dreams, sometimes I used to see vast dark waters opening up before me. But I've never dreamed, no one has ever dreamed, of water as dark as this, which was right in front my eyes. It was the darkest, most desolate water in the world. Around the lake there was nothing except tall, black, barren rocks. Birds circled over the murky water, many birds. You couldn't see them, but you could hear them. I've never heard anything as sorrowful as their cries. Oh, I felt so sorry for them! They sounded as if they were calling for help. They sounded as if they were weeping and out of hope.

On the other side of the lake, on the tallest rock, stood a big black fortress. Only one window was lighted. It was like an evil eye, that window, an awful and terrible red evil eye, staring out into the night wanting to hurt us.

Sir Kato's castle! He was over there, on the other side of the dark water lived my enemy, whom I had come to fight. The evil eye staring over the lake scared me, although I had made up my mind not to be scared. It scared me—how could anyone as small as I conquer one as evil and dangerous as Sir Kato?

"You need a sword," said Pompoo.

Just as he spoke we heard someone moaning nearby.

"Oh…oh…oh," the voice moaned. "I'm dying of hunger, oh…oh…oh!"

I knew it would be dangerous to approach. It could be someone trying to lure us into a trap. But whoever it was, I had to look for him and find out if he really needed help.

"We must see who it is," I said to Pompoo. "We must help him."

"I'm coming with you," said Pompoo.

"And you, Miramis, stay here," I said stroking his nose. He neighed anxiously.

"Don't worry," I said. "We'll be right back."

Whoever moaned couldn't be far away, but it would still be hard to find him in the dark.

"Oh...oh...oh," we heard again. "I'm dying of hunger, oh...oh...oh!"

We stumbled along the way toward the moaning voice, we tripped over stones and fell down in the dark, but at last we found an old cottage. It was a shack really. If it hadn't been leaning against a rock wall, it would have fallen down. We saw a dim light in one window and we crept up and peeked inside. An old man sat inside, a gaunt, pitiful little old man with tousled gray hair. He had a fire in the fireplace, and he sat in front of the fire, rocking back and forth saying, "Oh...oh... oh, I'm dying of hunger, oh...oh...oh!"

Then we went in. The little old man became quiet and stared at us. We stood there in the doorway and he stared at us as if he'd never seen anyone like us before. He held up his scrawny old hands as if he was scared.

"Don't hurt me," he whispered. "Don't hurt me!"

I said that we hadn't come to hurt him. "We heard you say you were hungry," I said. "We've come to give you bread."

I took out the bread, that I got from the Weaver, and passed it to the old man. He stared at me just as before. I held the bread even closer to him, but he still looked scared, awfully scared, as if he thought that I was luring him into a trap.

Mio, My Son

"Take the bread," I said. "Don't be scared!"

Then he cautiously stretched out his hand and took it. He took it in his hands and felt it. Then he put it up to his nose and smelled it. And then he began to cry.

"It's bread," he whispered. "It's Bread That Satisfies Hunger."

And so he ate. Never have I seen anyone eat like that. He ate and ate and cried while he ate. When he finished, he picked up every little crumb that had fallen on his clothes. He searched and searched until there was nothing left to find, then he stared at us again and said, "Where did you come from? Where did you get bread like this? Think of all my days of hunger—tell me where you got it."

"We come from Farawayland. That's where the bread came from," I said.

"Why have you come here?" whispered the old man.

"To fight Sir Kato," I said.

The moment I said this, the old man shrieked and fell off his stool. Just like a little gray ball of wool, he rolled down onto the floor and came crawling over to us. He stayed by our feet, peering up with his small wary eyes.

"Go back to where you came from," he whispered. "Go back before it's too late."

"I won't go back," I said. "I've come to fight Sir Kato."

I said it loudly and clearly. I said Sir Kato's name as sharply and clearly as I could, and the old man stared at me as if he believed I would fall down dead right in front of him.

"Oh…oh…oh," he moaned. "Be quiet! Be quiet and go back to where you came from. Go, before it's too late, I say."

"I will not go back," I said. "I have come to fight Sir Kato."

"Shhh," whispered the old man, and he looked completely frightened out of his wits. "I said be quiet. The spies may hear you. Maybe they're lurking outside right now."

He crawled to the door and listened anxiously. "I don't hear anyone there," he said. "But they could still be there. They could be here, they could be there, or everywhere. Spies every…everywhere."

"Sir Kato's spies?" I asked.

"Be quiet, boy," whispered the old man. "Are you so willing to lose your young life? Can't you keep quiet?"

He sat down on the stool and nodded to himself. "Yes, yes," he said, so quietly that you could hardly hear him. "His spies are everywhere, morning, noon and night. Always everywhere."

He stretched out his hand and took my arm. "Because of all my days of hunger," he whispered, "I don't trust anyone. You go into a house…you think you're among friends. But you're among enemies. They betray you. They hand you over to the one who lives on the other side of the lake. Trust no one. Don't trust me! How do you know that I won't set the spies on you the moment you're out the door?"

"I don't believe you'll do that," I said.

"No one can be certain," whispered the old man. "You can never be sure."

He sat quietly for a moment and thought.

"No, I won't set the spies on you," he said. "There are still a few people in this land who aren't traitors. And there are still some who forge weapons."

"We need a weapon," said Pompoo. "Mio needs a sword."

The old man didn't answer. He went to the window and opened it. And from across the lake you could hear the birds' sad cries. It sounded as if they wept out there, in the dark night.

"Listen," the old man said to me. "Do you hear how they wail? Do you want to be one who flies wailing over the lake, too?"

"What kind of birds are they?" I asked.

"They are the Bewitched Birds," whispered the old man. "You know well enough who bewitched them. You know well enough who captured them. And now you know what happens to those who try to fight thieves."

I was so sad when I heard what he said. The birds—they were Nonno's brothers and Totty's sister and the

Weaver's little daughter and all the others that Sir Kato had captured and bewitched. Oh, I would fight him—I would indeed!

"Mio needs a sword," said Pompoo. "No one can fight without a sword."

"You said there are some who forge weapons," I reminded the old man.

He stared at me, almost angrily. "You're not afraid of losing your young life," he said.

"Where are those who forge weapons?" I asked again.

"Be quiet," said the old man, and he hastily shut the window. "Be quiet, the spies may hear you."

He crept over to the door and put his ear next to it and listened.

"I don't hear anyone there," he said. "But they could be there anyway. Spies everywhere."

He leaned toward me and whispered in my ear, "You must go to the Swordsmith and tell him Eno sent you. You must say that you need a sword which can cut through stone. You must say that you're a knight from Farawayland." He looked at me for a long time. "For I believe that's what you are," he said. "Aren't you?"

"Yes," Pompoo answered for me. "He's a knight and a prince. Prince Mio from Farawayland. And he must have a sword."

"Where can I find the Swordsmith?" I asked.

"In the Deepest Cave in the Blackest Mountain," said the old man. "Go through the Dead Forest! Go now!"

He went to the window and opened it again. And from out over the lake, I once more heard the birds wailing in the night.

"Go now, Prince Mio," said the old man. "I will sit here and wish that all goes well with you. But perhaps I'll hear a new bird tomorrow night, flying over the lake and wailing."

In the Dead Forest

JUST AS WE closed Eno's door behind us, I heard Miramis neigh. He neighed so loudly and desperately. He seemed to be calling, "Mio, come and help me!"

My heart almost stopped, I was so scared. "Pompoo, what are they doing with Miramis?" I screamed. "Can you hear? What are they doing with Miramis?"

"Quiet," said Pompoo. "They've caught him…the spies…."

"How did the spies find Miramis?" I screamed, not caring if anyone heard me.

"You must be quiet," whispered Pompoo. "Or else they'll catch us, too."

But I didn't listen to what he said. Miramis, my own horse! It was my own horse they were taking away from me! And he was the kindest and most beautiful horse in the world.

I heard him neigh again and thought it was exactly as if he cried, "Mio, can't you help me?"

"Come," said Pompoo, "we must see what they're doing with him."

Mio, My Son

We climbed over the rocks in the darkness. We scrambled and climbed. I cut my fingers on the sharp edges, but I didn't feel it. I was worried for Miramis's sake.

He stood high on a rock and he shone white in the darkness. My Miramis, the brightest and most beautiful horse in the world!

He neighed wildly and reared, trying to break loose. But five black spies stood around him, and two of them were hanging on to his bridle. Poor Miramis was so

scared, and it wasn't surprising. Because the black spies were so horrible and they talked to each other with their horrible raspy voices. Pompoo and I crept as close

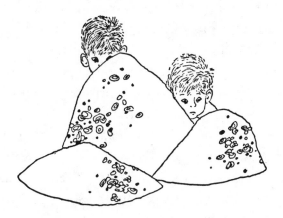

as we could and hid behind some rocks and heard what the spies were saying.

"The best thing is to take him back over the Dead Lake in the black boat," said one of them.

"Yes, straight across the Dead Lake to Sir Kato," said another.

I wanted to shout at them to leave my horse alone, but I didn't. Who would fight Sir Kato if I was captured by the spies? Oh, why must *I* be the one who would fight Sir Kato? I regretted it terribly, as I hid behind the rocks. Why hadn't I stayed at home with my father the King, where no one could take my horse from me! I heard the Bewitched Birds wailing out over the lake, but I didn't care about them. I didn't care about them at all. They could continue being bewitched, if only I got back my Miramis with the golden mane.

"Someone must have crossed the border," said one of the spies. "Someone must have been riding on the white colt. The enemy is among us."

"Good, the enemy is among us," said another. "It'll be so much easier to capture him. So much easier for Sir Kato to crush him and destroy him."

I trembled when I heard them. I was the enemy who had crossed the border. I was the one Sir Kato would crush and destroy. I regretted even more that I had come here. And I missed my father the King so much and wondered if he missed me too, and was worried about me. I wish that he'd been there and could help me. I wish that I could've talked to him for a little while. Then I would have said to him, "I know you want me to fight Sir Kato, but won't you please let me off? Help me get Miramis back and let us leave! You know I've never had my own horse before and I love him. You also know I've never had a father either. And if Sir Kato captures me, I will never be with you again. Help me leave! I don't want to be here any more. I want to be with you. I want to go home again to Greenfields Island with Miramis."

As I was hiding behind the rocks, I thought I heard my father the King's voice. Of course I only imagined it, but I thought that I heard his voice.

"Mio, my son," he said.

Nothing more. But I understood that he wanted me to be brave and not lie there crying and screaming like a child, even though they took my Miramis away from me. I was a knight. I was no longer the Mio that built huts in the Garden of Roses and wandered over the hills on Greenfields Island playing the flute. I was a knight, a *good* knight, not one like Sir Kato. And a knight must be brave and not cry.

So I didn't cry, although I saw the spies lead Miramis down to the lake and force him on a large black boat. I didn't cry, but Miramis neighed as if they had whipped him. I didn't cry when the spies took the oars and I heard the oars beating across the dark water. It sounded fainter and fainter, and I heard Miramis's last desperate neigh far out on the lake, finally the boat disappeared from sight—but I didn't cry. Because I was a knight.

Didn't I cry? Yes, that's just what I did. I lay there behind the rocks with my forehead against the hard ground and cried more than I had done in all my life. A good knight must speak the truth. And it was true that I cried. For Miramis's sake. I cried and cried and when I thought of his faithful eyes, I cried even more. The Weaver had said that the hundred white horses wept tears of blood for the foal that was stolen. Maybe it was blood that I cried for Miramis too, who knows? It was so dark that I couldn't see. My Miramis with the golden mane! He was gone, and I might never see him again.

Pompoo bent down and put his hand on my shoulder.

"Don't cry any more, Mio," he said. "We must go see the Swordsmith. You need a sword."

There were many more tears left in me, but I held them back. I took a deep breath. And we went to find the Swordsmith.

"Go through the Dead Forest," Eno had said. But where was the Dead Forest?

"We must find the Swordsmith before night is over," I said to Pompoo. "The darkness hides us from

the spies. We must hurry through the Dead Forest tonight."

We climbed back over the rocks to Eno's cottage. It stood dark and silent, and no one moaned inside any longer. We went on through the night and at last we came to the Dead Forest. It was a forest where no wind whistled and no leaves rustled, because there were no little green leaves. There were only dead, black tree trunks with dead, gnarled, black branches.

"Now we've reached the Dead Forest," said Pompoo as we walked between the trees.

"Yes, we've entered it," I said, "but I don't believe we'll ever leave it."

It was a forest to easily become lost in. It was the type of forest in dreams, where you walk and walk and never find the way out.

We held each other's hands, Pompoo and I, as we walked through the Dead Forest, and we felt very small and lost. The dead trees stood so close, we could hardly move.

"If only the trees hadn't grown so close together," said Pompoo. "If only the darkness weren't so black and we weren't so small and alone!"

We walked and walked. Sometimes we heard voices far away. It was the spies that we heard. What Eno had said was probably true, that Sir Kato's spies were every-where. The entire Dead Forest was certainly full of

them. And when we heard them far away among the trees, we stood so still, Pompoo and I, and hardly dared to breathe.

We walked and walked.

"The night is certainly long here in the Dead Forest," said Pompoo. "But the way to the Swordsmith's cave will certainly take even longer."

"Pompoo, do you believe we'll find him…" I began. But then I fell silent. I couldn't say a word more, because toward us, from between the trees, came a line of black spies. They came straight toward us, and I knew it was the end. Pompoo saw them too, and he squeezed my hand so hard. They hadn't seen us yet, but soon they would be upon us, and that would be the end. I would never get to fight Sir Kato. And tomorrow

night Eno would hear two new birds wailing as they flew over the lake.

Closer and closer came the spies, and we stood there and waited and they still hadn't found us. But then something strange happened. An old black tree trunk right next to us opened up, and I saw that it was hollow. Before I knew how it happened, we crept inside the hollow trunk, Pompoo and I, and sat there trembling like two baby birds hunted by the hawk. Now the spies were close to us and we heard what they said.

"I heard someone talking in the Dead Forest," said one of them. "Who is speaking in the Dead Forest?"

"The enemy is among us," said another. "It must be the enemy that speaks in the Dead Forest."

"If the enemy is in the Dead Forest, we'll find him soon," said another. "Search! Search everywhere!"

We heard them searching and looking among the trees. We heard their furtive steps outside, and we crouched there, feeling so small and scared.

They looked and looked, but they didn't find us. Their voices sounded farther and farther away. At last it was silent. The hollow tree had saved us.

Why had the tree saved us? I didn't understand it. Was it because the entire Dead Forest hated Sir Kato and would gladly help the one who had come to fight him? Maybe this dead tree had once been a healthy young tree covered with small green leaves that rustled as the wind swept through its branches. Sir Kato's evilness must have made them wither and die. I don't think a tree can ever forgive someone who has killed its small green leaves. That's probably why this tree wanted to help the one who had come to fight Sir Kato.

"Thank you, kind tree," I said, as we crept out of the hollow trunk.

But the tree stood silent and dead and didn't answer.

We walked and walked through the Dead Forest.

"Dawn is here," said Pompoo, "and we haven't found the Swordsmith's cave."

Yes, night was over. But the dawn wasn't light and bright as it was at home. The dawn here was an ugly gray which was almost like the night. I remembered the sunrise at home on Greenfields Island when we rode on Miramis and the grass was wet with dew, so that every little blade glittered. I walked and thought of Miramis and almost forgot where I was. So I wasn't at all surprised or frightened when I heard the sound of approaching hooves. "Here comes Miramis," I thought. But Pompoo grabbed my arm and whispered, "Listen! The spies are riding through the Dead Forest."

Then I knew the end had come. No one could save us now. Soon we would see the black spies coming from between the trees, and they would see *us*. They would come riding like the wind, and just bend down and seize us and throw us up on their horses and sweep on to Sir Kato's castle. I would never get to fight him. And tomorrow night Eno would hear two new birds wailing as they flew over the lake.

This was the end. I knew it. Closer and closer came the hoofbeats. But then something strange happened. A hole in the ground opened before us, and I saw a burrow there. Before I knew how it happened, Pompoo and I crawled down in a crowded heap into the burrow, trembling like two baby rabbits hunted by the fox.

We were just in time. We heard hoofbeats coming closer. We heard the spies riding above us, right over our burrow. We heard the trampling of hooves, we heard the horses' heavy feet thunder across the earth above our heads. A little bit of the dirt loosened and trickled down on us. And we crouched there feeling so small and scared.

But it became quiet. As quiet as if there weren't any spies in the Dead Forest. We waited longer.

"I think we can crawl out now," I said at last.

But just then we heard the horrible sound of hooves again. The spies were coming back. Once more the hooves thundered over our heads, and we heard the spies shouting and yelling. They jumped off their horses and sat down on the ground just outside the burrow. We could see them through the opening. They were so close we could've touched them. And we could hear them talking.

"Orders from Sir Kato that the enemy must be captured," said one of them. "The enemy who rode on the white colt must be captured tonight. It's Sir Kato's command."

"The enemy is in our midst," said another, "and we'll certainly capture him. Search! Search everywhere!"

They were sitting very close to us, speaking about how they would catch us. Dark and terrifying, they sat there in the sinister gray light, with all the dead trees around them and their black horses snapping wildly and stamping the ground.

"Search! Search everywhere!" said a spy. "What is that hole in the ground there?"

"A burrow," said another. "Maybe the enemy is inside there. Search everywhere!"

Pompoo and I held each other tightly. This was the end, I knew it.

"I'll prod with my spear," said one of the spies. "If the enemy is in there I'll pierce him with my spear."

We saw a black spear coming through the entrance. We had crept as far back into the burrow as we could go. But the spear was long, the sharp point came closer and closer. The spear thrust and thrust. But it didn't hit us. It hit the wall of the burrow between Pompoo and me, but it didn't hit us.

"Search! Search the entire Dead Forest," said the

spies outside. "Orders from Sir Kato that the enemy must be caught. But he isn't here. Search everywhere!"

So the spies mounted their black horses and rode away.

We were safe. The burrow had rescued us, and I wondered why. Was it because even the earth and the ground hated Sir Kato and would gladly help the one who had come to fight him? Maybe soft green grass had once grown on this ground, wet from the dew at dawn. Sir Kato's evilness must have made it wither and die. I don't believe the ground can ever forgive anyone who has killed the soft green grass that once grew there. That must be why the earth protected the one who had come to fight Sir Kato.

"Thank you, kind earth," I said, when we left. But the earth didn't answer. It lay silent, and the burrow was gone.

We walked and walked, and reached the end of the Dead Forest. Mountains and cliffs rose up in front of us. I felt hopeless. We had come back to the rocks around the Dead Lake. We felt so hopeless, Pompoo and I. It was no good going on. We would never find the Swordsmith. We had been walking through the Dead Forest for the whole night, and now we were back exactly where we had started. Eno's cottage stood there, small and gray and shabby. It leaned against the cliff so it wouldn't fall down. It was a tall, jet black cliff that it leaned against.

"This must be the blackest mountain in the world," said Pompoo.

The blackest mountain—yes, of course that's where the Swordsmith was supposed to have his cave! "The Deepest Cave in the Blackest Mountain," Eno had said.

"Oh, Pompoo," I began. "You'll see…"

I stopped. And I knew that the end had come, because now a long, long line of black spies came

storming out of the Dead Forest. Some came running, some came charging on black horses, and they all came straight toward us. They had seen us, and they shouted loudly with their horrible raspy voices.

"The enemy is in our midst. There he is! Capture him! Capture him! Orders from Sir Kato that the enemy must be caught."

We stood there, Pompoo and I, with our backs against the cliff and we saw the spies coming closer and closer. Yes, the end had come! I would never fight Sir Kato. I became very sad. I wanted to lie down on the ground and cry. Tomorrow night Eno would hear a bird flying over the lake, a bird that wailed louder and more sorrowfully than all the others. And Eno would stand by his window, murmuring to himself, "Out there flies Prince Mio."

The Deepest Cave
in the Blackest Mountain

BUT THEN SOMETHING strange happened. The cliff we
were pressing against gave way and before we knew how
it happened, we were standing inside the mountain,
Pompoo and I, trembling like two lambs hunted by the
wolf.

We didn't need to be scared. We were inside the
mountain and the spies were outside. The cliff had
closed, there was no opening. They could never catch
us here. But we heard them raging outside.

"Search! Search everywhere!" they shouted. "The enemy was in our midst, but now he's vanished. Search everywhere!"

"Yes, you search," I said. "You'll never find us here."

We were so glad, Pompoo and I, and we laughed loudly inside the mountain. But I thought of Miramis and then I didn't laugh anymore.

We looked around. We were in a big cave. It was dark, but not completely dark. We saw a faint light, but couldn't tell where it came from. Many dark passages led from the cave farther into the mountain.

"In the Deepest Cave in the Blackest Mountain lives the Swordsmith," Eno had said. Maybe one of the dark passages led to the Swordsmith, but which one? We didn't know. We would probably have to walk for a long time before we found him.

"Well anyway, now we're inside the Blackest Mountain," said Pompoo.

"We're definitely inside," I said, "but I don't think we'll ever find the way out again."

Because it was a mountain to easily become lost in, it was the kind of mountain you dream about sometimes. You walk and you walk in strange, dark passages and never find the way out.

Hand in hand Pompoo and I walked farther into the mountain. We felt so small and confused, and it was probably a long way to the Deepest Cave.

"If only the mountain weren't so scary," said Pompoo. "If only the passages weren't so dark and if we weren't so small and alone."

We walked and walked. The passage divided. It branched out in every direction. A whole network of dark passages led into the mountain. Sometimes the faint light grew a bit stronger, so we could see a few yards in front of us, but sometimes it was so dark we couldn't see anything at all. Sometimes the passage was so low that we couldn't stand straight, sometimes the ceiling was as high as in a church. The mountain walls were damp with water, it was cold, and we wrapped our cloaks tighter around us so we wouldn't freeze.

"Maybe we'll never find the way out and never find the Swordsmith's cave," said Pompoo.

We were hungry and we ate a little of the Bread That Satisfies Hunger. We only ate a little, because we didn't know how long it must last.

We continued walking while we ate. When I had finished my bread, we came to a place where the passage split into three different paths.

Water ran down the wall of the passage and I was thirsty. I stopped and drank the water. It didn't taste good, but there wasn't any other. When I was done I turned to Pompoo. But Pompoo wasn't there. He was gone. Maybe he hadn't noticed that I stopped for a drink and so he continued along one of the passages, thinking I was close behind him.

At first I wasn't scared. I stood there at the fork and wondered which way Pompoo had gone. He couldn't have gone more than a few steps, and all I had to do was shout to him.

"Pompoo, where are you?" I shouted as loudly as I could. But my cry only sounded like a ghostly whisper, I didn't know what kind of strange mountain this was. The rock walls deadened the sound of my voice and silenced it, so that it became a whisper. And the whispers came back, the whispers echoed in the mountain.

"Pompoo, where are you?" whispered the dark passages. "Pompoo, where are you...Pompoo, where are you?"

Then I became so scared. I tried to scream even louder, but the mountain only kept on whispering. I couldn't believe that it was my own voice I heard, but another's. One who was sitting far inside the mountain and mocking me.

"Pompoo, where are you...Pompoo, where are you...Pompoo, where are you?" it whispered.

Oh! I became so scared! I rushed into the left passage and ran a few steps, then I rushed back to the fork and ran to the right, turned back again, and rushed into the middle passage. "Pompoo, which way have you gone?" I dared not shout, because the whispering was so awful.

But I thought that Pompoo would know how terribly I missed him and wanted him to come back to me.

The passage divided again. There were new dark passages in every direction, and I ran here and there, looking and looking. I tried not to cry, because I was a knight. But I didn't have the energy to be a knight just then. I thought of Pompoo running somewhere else on another path, so worried and calling to me, and I laid down on the rough rocky floor and cried as much as when the spies took Miramis. Now I had no Miramis, and no Pompoo. I was all alone. I lay crying and regretting I had come here, and I didn't know how my father the King could have ever wanted me to go off and fight Sir Kato. I wished my father the King were here so that I could talk to him.

"Look, I'm all alone," I would have said. "Pompoo is gone and you know he's my best friend now that I don't have Ben any more. Now I don't have Pompoo either. I am all alone and it's only because you want me to fight Sir Kato."

For the first time I almost thought that my father

the King had been a little unfair wanting me to take such risks. But as I lay there crying it was like I really heard my father the King's voice. I know it was my imagination, but I really thought I heard him.

"Mio, my son," he said.

No more. But it sounded as if he meant there was nothing to be sad about. I thought that maybe I could find Pompoo, after all.

I rose up from the ground and something fell out of my pocket. It was the little wooden flute that Nonno had carved for me. My flute, that I had played around the campfire on Greenfields Island.

"I'll play my flute," I thought. "I'll play the old melody that Nonno taught us." I remembered what Pompoo and I had promised each other, "If we ever become separated, we'll play the old melody."

I put the flute to my mouth, but I hardly risked playing it. I was afraid nothing except an awful ghostly sound would come out, like when I shouted. But I thought I had to try. So I began to play the melody.

Oh! It sounded so clear! It sounded pure and clear and beautiful inside the dark mountain, almost better than it had on Greenfields Island.

I played the whole melody, and then I listened. From far, far away in the mountain clear notes came in reply. They sounded faint, but I knew it was Pompoo who answered me. I've never been so glad.

The Deepest Cave in the Blackest Mountain

I kept on playing, and although I was so happy, I couldn't stop crying. I went through the mountain, playing and crying a little. I only cried a little, little bit as I went through there and played, and I ran toward the sound of Pompoo's flute. Sometimes it sounded closer, and I tried to follow the direction that the notes came from. Closer and closer it sounded. Clearer and clearer, louder and louder I heard the old melody from the other flute like mine. And right then Pompoo stood in front of me in the dark passage. I stretched out my hand and touched him. I laid my arm on his shoulder. I wanted to make sure that it was really him. And it was. It was my very best friend.

"If I ever see Nonno again, I'll thank him for making these flutes for us," said Pompoo.

"I will too," I said.

But then I thought that we'd probably never see Nonno again.

"Pompoo, which way should we go now?" I said.

"It doesn't matter which way we go, as long as we go together," said Pompoo.

That's exactly what I thought too. We walked and walked, and we didn't feel so small and lost anymore. Because we were together and we played on our flutes. The old melody sounded clear and pretty in the Blackest Mountain, and it was as if it wanted to comfort us and help us to be brave.

Mio, My Son

The passage sloped downward, further and further
down. The faint light we had seen throughout the
mountain became a little brighter. It seemed to come
from a fire. Yes, the firelight shone over the dark rock
walls of the mountain, it flickered and grew.

We came closer and closer to the fire as we walked
and played our flutes. We played the old melody when
we stepped into the Swordsmith's Cave.

It was a smithy we had come to, and a huge fire
burned there. There was a big anvil and by the anvil
stood a man. He was probably the biggest and strongest
man I've ever seen. He had a lot of red hair and a big
red beard. He was sooty and black and had the biggest
and blackest hands that I've seen. He had thick, bushy
eyebrows, and when we stepped into his cave, he stood
still and looked at us with his eyebrows turned up in
great surprise.

"Who plays in my mountain?" he said. "Who is it
that plays in my mountain?"

"A knight accompanied by his squire," said Pompoo.
"A knight from Farawayland. Prince Mio is the one
who plays in your mountain."

The Swordsmith came toward me. He touched my
forehead with his sooty finger and looked astonished.

"How fair is your brow," he said. "How clear is
your eye! And how beautifully you play in my mountain!"

"I've come to ask you for a sword," I said. "Eno has sent me."

"What will you do with a sword?" said the Swordsmith.

"I will fight Sir Kato," I said.

As soon as I said that, the Swordsmith roared more terribly than I've ever heard before.

"Sir Kato!" he shrieked, so that it boomed inside the mountain. "Sir Kato, death to him!"

A thunderous rumble echoed far away in the dark passages. When the Swordsmith shouted it didn't become a whisper. No, it boomed and echoed louder than thunder between the rock walls.

The Swordsmith stood there with his big black hands clenched, and the light from the fire fell over his face, which was dark with rage.

"Sir Kato, death to him!" he shrieked over and over again.

The light from the fire also fell on a long row of sharp swords, hanging on the walls of his cave. They glittered and glimmered and looked so ghastly. I went to look at them. The Swordsmith stopped yelling and came over to me.

"Look at my swords," he said. "All of my sharp swords. I have forged them for Sir Kato. Sir Kato's swordsmith, that's who I am."

"If you're his swordsmith why did you shout 'Death to Sir Kato?' " I asked.

He clenched his hands so tightly that his knuckles became white. "Because no one hates Sir Kato as deeply as his own swordsmith," he said.

Then I noticed he dragged a long chain of iron that bound him to the mountain wall. It rattled as he walked across the floor.

"Why are you chained to the mountain?" I asked. "And why haven't you heated the chain over your fire and broken it on your anvil?"

"Sir Kato chained me here firmly, himself," said the Swordsmith. "No fire can break his chains and no hammer. Sir Kato's chains of hate don't break so easily."

"Why do you have to wear chains of hate?" I asked.

"Because I forge his swords," he said. "I forge the swords that kill the good and innocent. That's the reason Sir Kato has chained me firmly, with the most secure chains there are. He can't manage without my swords."

The Swordsmith looked at me with eyes that burned like fire. "I sit here in my cave hammering swords for Sir Kato. Night and day I hammer swords for him, he knows that. But there is one he doesn't know about, and this is it here."

The Swordsmith dragged his chains over to the cave's darkest corner and from a crevice he brought out a sword. It was shining like a flame of fire in his hand.

"For thousands and thousands of years I've hammered this sword, which can cut through stone," he said. "And now, tonight I've finally succeeded, not until this very night."

He lifted the sword and with a single slash cut a big gash in the mountain wall.

"Oh, my sword, my Flame of Fire," he muttered. "My sword which can cut through stone!"

"Why must you have a sword that can cut through stone?" I asked.

"I'll tell you," said the Swordsmith. "This sword was not forged for the good and innocent. This sword lies waiting for Sir Kato himself. He has a heart of stone. You didn't know?"

"No, I know very little about Sir Kato," I said. "I only know that I've come to fight him."

"He has a heart of stone," said the Swordsmith, "and a claw of iron."

"He has a claw of iron?" I said.

"You didn't know?" said the Swordsmith. "His right hand is gone and in its place he has a claw of iron."

"What does he do with his claw of iron?" I asked.

"He tears the heart out of people's chests," said the Swordsmith. "Only one touch from the iron claw—instantly the heart is gone. Then he gives them a heart of stone in its place. Everyone around him must have a heart of stone, so he decided."

I shivered when I heard that. And more and more I began to wish it were finally time to fight Sir Kato.

The Swordsmith stood beside me. He stroked the sword with his sooty hands. It was certainly his most precious possession.

"Give me your sword that cuts through stone," I requested. "Give me your sword so that I can fight Sir Kato."

The Swordsmith stood silent for a long time and looked at me. "Yes, you may have my sword," he said at last. "You may have my Flame of Fire. Only because your brow is so fair and your eye so clear and because you played so beautifully in my mountain."

He placed the flaming sword in my hand and fire seemed to flow from it right through my whole body, making me so strong.

Then the Swordsmith walked toward the wall of the cave and opened a large hole. I felt a cold, icy wind flow in and heard the sound of crashing waves.

"Sir Kato knows much," said the Swordsmith. "But he doesn't know that I've bored through the mountain and opened my prison. I drilled for many years so that I could have a window in my prison."

I walked over to the hole and looked out across the Dead Lake toward Sir Kato's castle. It was night again, and the castle lay as dark and sinister as it had when I last saw it. And just as before, one window glared like an evil eye out over the water of the Dead Lake.

Pompoo came over beside me, and we stood there quietly and thought of the approaching fight.

The Swordsmith was behind us and I heard his voice. "It's coming, it's coming," he murmured. "Sir Kato's final battle approaches."

A Claw of Iron

THE SKY ABOVE the lake was dark, and the air was filled with the Bewitched Birds' cries. Out there were the dark frothy waves, the frothy waves that would cast our boat across the Dead Lake and maybe strike it against the rocks below Sir Kato's castle.

The Swordsmith stood by the opening and watched while I untied a little boat. It lay moored in a cove inside the mountain itself, a cove hidden between high walls of rock.

"Sir Kato knows much," said the Swordsmith, "but he doesn't know that the Dead Lake dug into my mountain. He knows nothing about my secret cove and nothing about the boat that lies by the secret landing under my window."

"Why do you have a boat that you can never row?" I asked.

"I can row," said the Swordsmith. "I climb out through this opening and stretch my chain as far as it goes. Then I can row. I can row three boat-lengths in my secret cove."

He stood by the opening, big and black he loomed above the landing. It was so dark that I could hardly see him, but I could hear him laughing. It was a strange, frightening laugh. It was as if he didn't really know how to laugh.

"Sir Kato knows much," he said. "But there is something else he doesn't know. He doesn't know what is loaded in my boat that will cross the Dead Lake tonight."

"And there is something *you* don't know," I said. "You don't know if you will ever see your boat again. Maybe it will lie at the bottom of the lake tonight. Like a cradle rocked by the waves, at the bottom of the Dead Lake perhaps, and in the cradle sleep Pompoo and I. What will you say then?"

The Swordsmith sighed deeply.

"Then I'll just say, 'Sleep soundly, Prince Mio! Sleep soundly in your cradle, rocked by the waves!'"

I began to row and lost sight of the Swordsmith. He disappeared in the darkness. But he called to us. Just as we steered through the narrow channel between the Swordsmith's secret cove and the Dead Lake, I heard him calling softly to us, "Be on your guard, Prince Mio," he called. "Be on your guard as soon as you see the claw of iron. If you don't have your sword ready then, it will be the end of Prince Mio."

"The end of Prince Mio...the end of Prince Mio,"

whispered the rock walls around us, and it sounded so eerie. But I didn't have time to think about it anymore, because at that moment the Dead Lake hurled wild waves across our boat and carried it far away from the Swordsmith's mountain.

We traveled over the surging depths. We were already far from land, and we felt so small and scared, Pompoo and I.

"If only our boat weren't so little," said Pompoo. "If only the lake weren't so deep and the waves so wild, and if we weren't so small and alone!"

Oh, how wild they were, all the waves in the Dead Lake! I've never seen wilder waves. They threw themselves over us, tore at us, pulled at us, and hurled us on toward more raging waves. It was pointless trying to row. We held on to the oars, both Pompoo and I. We held on as hard as we could. But a surging wave came and tore one of them from us, and another raging wave broke the second oar. Many violent spitting, surging waves rose sky-high around us and around our boat, which was frail and small, exactly as we were.

"Now we don't have any oars," said Pompoo. "And soon we won't have a boat. When the waves hurl it against Sir Kato's rocks it'll break. Then we'll never need a boat again."

The Bewitched Birds came flying from all directions. They circled around us and cried and wailed. They flew so close. I could see their blank, melancholy little eyes in the darkness.

"Are you Nonno's brother?" I asked one of them. "Are you Totty's little sister?" I asked another.

But they only looked at me with their blank, melancholy little eyes, and their cries were cries of despair.

Though we didn't have oars and our boat was crippled, we were carried straight toward Sir Kato's castle. That was where the waves wanted to take us, it was there they thought of crushing us against the rocks. We would die at Sir Kato's feet, as the waves wanted.

We came closer and closer to the dangerous rocks, closer and closer to the black castle with the evil staring eye, faster and faster the boat went, wilder and wilder were the waves.

"Now," said Pompoo, "now...Oh, Mio, it's the end!"

But then something strange happened. Just as we thought we would die, the waves calmed down and became still. They became completely still. They carried our boat gently past all the dangerous reefs and pushed it gently toward the black rugged rocks below Sir Kato's castle.

Why had the waves surged so wildly at first and then grown still? I didn't understand it. Maybe it was because they hated Sir Kato and gladly wanted to help the one who had come to fight him. Maybe the Dead Lake had once been a happy and blue little lake lying between safe shores, a little lake that reflected the sunshine on beautiful summer days and where gentle little waves splashed against the rocks. Maybe there was a time when children swam and played on the shores and the sound of children's laughter rang out across the water, not sounding like it did now with the Bewitched Birds' sad cries. That was probably why the waves had rushed high around us, and why they had made a frothy barrier between us and the evil staring eye in the castle up above.

"Thank you, kind lake!" I said. "Thank you, wild waves!"

But there were no waves. The water lay still and quiet and black, not answering.

High over our heads, high above on the steep cliff stood Sir Kato's castle. We were on his shore now. We were close to him as never before, and this night was the night of our battle. I wondered if they knew, all those who had waited for thousands and thousands of years. I wondered if they knew that this was the night of the battle, and if they thought about me. Was my father the King thinking of me? I hoped that he was. I knew that he was. I knew that he was sitting alone somewhere far away and thinking of me and was sad and whispering to himself, "Mio, my son!"

I grasped my sword and it felt like fire in my hand. It was a terrible battle that I had to fight, and I didn't want to wait any longer. I longed to meet Sir Kato, even if it meant I would die. The promised battle must be now, even if there wouldn't be a Mio anymore when it was over.

"Mio, I'm so hungry," said Pompoo.

I took out what was left of the Bread That Satisfies Hunger and we ate it by the rocks below Sir Kato's castle. Our hunger was satisfied, we felt stronger and almost happy after we had eaten it. But it was the last of our bread and we didn't know when we would have more to eat.

"Now we must climb the cliff," I said to Pompoo. "It's the only way for us to reach Sir Kato's castle."

"I suppose it is," said Pompoo.

So we began climbing up the cliff, which rose so high and was awfully steep.

"If only the rocks weren't so steep," said Pompoo. "If only the night weren't so dark and we weren't so small and alone."

We climbed and climbed. It took so long and it was so dark. But we clung firmly with our hands and feet, we looked for crevices and outcroppings, we held on and kept climbing. Sometimes I was so scared and believed that I couldn't go on and that I would fall down, that it would be the end. But at the last moment I always found something to hold. It was as if the rocks themselves stuck a small ledge under my foot when

I started to fall. Maybe even the rocks hated Sir Kato and gladly wanted to help the one who had come to fight him.

Sky-high over the water stood Sir Kato's castle, and sky-high we climbed to reach the castle wall, which was at the top of the cliff.

"Soon we'll be there," I whispered to Pompoo. "Soon we'll climb over the wall, and then...."

I heard voices! The spies were talking to each other in the darkness, two black spies that kept watch up on the wall.

"Search! Search everywhere!" said one of them. "Orders from Sir Kato that the enemy must be captured. The enemy who rode on the white colt must be caught. It is Sir Kato's command. Search the caves in the mountains, search among the trees of the forest, search on the water and in the air, search near and far, search everywhere!"

"Search near, search near!" said the other. "We search near. Maybe the enemy is among us. Maybe he climbs up the cliff tonight. Search everywhere!"

My heart nearly stopped beating when I saw him light a torch. If his torch shone below the wall, he would see us. And if he saw us, it would be the end. He would only need to reach out his long spear and give us a push. Then he'd never need to search again for the enemy who rode on the white colt. There would just be a little cry as we tumbled down into the Dead Lake and vanished forever.

"Search! Search everywhere!" said one of the spies. "Shine your torch over the castle wall. Maybe the enemy is climbing up right now. Search everywhere!"

The other lifted the torch in his hand and leaned out over the wall. The light fell on the face of the cliff and we huddled together and trembled like two mice hunted by the cat. The light from the torch came closer, it crept along the wall and came closer and closer.

"Now," whispered Pompoo, "now...Oh, Mio, it's the end!"

But then something strange happened. Out from across the lake flew a flock of birds. All the Bewitched Birds swept in on rushing wings. One of them rushed straight toward the torch and it fell from the spy's hand. We saw a streak of fire falling down through the air, and we heard a hissing sound as the torch went out and sank into the lake. But down toward the water fell another streak of fire. The bird who had saved us was on fire. With flaming wings it sank into the waves of the Dead Lake.

We were so sad about the bird.

"Thank you, poor little bird," I whispered, although I knew the bird couldn't hear and would never hear anything more.

I wanted to cry for the bird, but I was forced to

think of the spies now. We still weren't over the wall, many dangers still awaited us.

The spies were so angry at the bird. They stood on the wall just above us. I could see their horrible black hoods and hear their hoarse voices as they whispered secretively to each other.

"Search! Search everywhere!" they said. "Maybe the enemy is farther away; maybe he is climbing the castle wall somewhere else. Search everywhere!"

They walked a few steps and looked in another direction.

"Now!" I whispered to Pompoo. "Now!"

We climbed over the wall. So quickly, so quickly we climbed over the wall; so quickly, so quickly we ran in the darkness toward Sir Kato's castle. We pressed against the black wall of the castle and stood still, frightened the spies would find us.

"How can we get into Sir Kato's castle?" whispered Pompoo. "How can we get into the blackest castle in the world?"

As soon as he said this, a door opened in the wall— a black door opened silently beside us. Not a sound was heard. The silence was vast and terrible, as no other silence. If only the door had creaked at least once when it opened! If the hinges had squeaked slightly, then it wouldn't have been so frightening. But this was the most silent of all doors.

Pompoo and I walked hand in hand into Sir Kato's castle. And we felt small and scared as never before.

No darkness was ever this sinister, no cold so bitter, no silence as evil as in Sir Kato's castle.

From the door a small, dark, winding stairway led upward. It was the tallest and darkest stairway I'd ever seen.

"If only the darkness weren't so frightening," whispered Pompoo. "If only Sir Kato weren't so cruel and we weren't so small and alone."

I gripped my sword and we crept up the stairs; I went first and Pompoo followed.

In my dreams, sometimes I used to walk through a dark house—an unknown, dark, frightening house. I was shut in a black room, so that I couldn't breathe, and the floor opened up to swallow me into its black depths, and the stairs gave way so that I fell. But the house in my dreams was not as scary as Sir Kato's castle.

We walked and walked up the winding stairs, and we didn't know what we'd find at the top.

"Mio, I'm scared," whispered Pompoo behind me. I turned to take his hand, but at that moment Pompoo disappeared. He disappeared through the wall without me understanding how it happened. I was left alone on the stairs, a thousand times more alone than when we lost each other in the Swordsmith's mountain, a thousand times more alone than ever before. I didn't dare shout, but with trembling hands I felt the surface of the wall where Pompoo disappeared. I cried and whispered, "Pompoo, where are you? Pompoo, come back!"

But the wall was cold and hard under my hands. There wasn't a crack that Pompoo could have slipped through. And all was quiet, as before. No Pompoo answered, while I whispered and wept, all was quiet.

Surely no one in the world was as alone as I, when I started back up the stairs. Surely no one's steps were as heavy as mine. I had almost no energy to lift my feet, and the steps were so tall and there were so many.

So many, but one of them was the last. I didn't know it was the last. I didn't know which step was at the end, I didn't know, as I went up the stairs in the darkness. I took a step and nothing was under my foot. I screamed and fell, and as I fell I tried to find something to hold on to. As I fell, I managed to catch hold of the top step. I hung there, struggling and feeling with my feet for something to stand on. But there was nothing. I was hanging over a black bottomless pit. I was so scared and there was no one to help. Soon I'll fall down, I thought, and it will be the end.... "Oh! Help me someone, help me!" I cried.

Someone came up the stairs. Was it Pompoo?

"Pompoo, please Pompoo, help me!" I whispered.

I couldn't see him, it was so dark. I couldn't see his kind face and his eyes that were like Ben's.

"Yes, yes. Take my hand, and I will help you," whispered the one I believed was Pompoo. "Take my hand, and I will help you!"

And I took his hand. But it was not a hand. It was a claw of iron!

I Never Saw a More
Fearsome Sword in My Castle

IN TIME I may forget him. In time I may forget Sir
Kato. I will forget his terrible face and his terrible eyes
and his terrible claw of iron. I long for that day, when
I won't remember him any more. Then I will be able
to forget his dreadful room, too.

He had a room in his castle where the air was thick
with evil. Because it was the room where Sir Kato sat
night and day and conceived his evil plans. Night and
day, night and day he sat there and plotted. The air was
so full of evil that no one could breathe in his room.
This evilness flowed swiftly outside, killing all that was
beautiful and alive and it withered away all the green
leaves and flowers and soft grass. It spread, an evil veil

across the sun, so that there was no real day but only night, or something like night. It's not surprising that the window of this room blazed like an evil eye over the waters of the Dead Lake. Sir Kato's evil blazed through the window as he worked on his vile plans. Night and day, night and day he sat there and plotted.

It was to this room that I was brought. Sir Kato had caught me when I needed both hands to hold myself up, and couldn't use my sword. His black spies seized me and dragged me to his room. Pompoo already stood there. He was so pale and weak, and he whispered, "Oh, Mio, it's the end."

Sir Kato came in and we saw his cruelty. We stood before his horrible face, he was silent and just stared at us. And his evilness ran over us like an icy river and his evilness crept over us like a burning fire, then it crept over our faces and our hands and stung our eyes, and it flowed down into our lungs as we tried to breathe. I felt his cruelty wash over me and I became so tired and I did not have enough strength left to lift my sword no matter how hard I tried. The spies passed my sword to Sir Kato and he caught his breath when he saw it.

"I never saw a more fearsome sword in my castle," he said to the spies as he looked around.

He went over to the window and stood there weighing the sword in his hand.

"What shall I do with this sword?" said Sir Kato. "The good and the innocent will not die from this sword. What shall I do with it?"

He watched me with cruel eyes and he saw how much I longed for my sword.

"I will sink this sword in the Dead Lake," said Sir Kato. "I will sink it in the deepest part of the Dead Lake, for I have never ever seen a more fearsome sword in my castle."

He lifted the sword and hurled it out the window. I saw it spinning through the air and I was heartbroken. For thousands and thousands of years the Swordsmith had forged this sword which could cut through stone. For thousands and thousands of years people had waited, hoping that I would vanquish Sir Kato. And now he was throwing my sword into the Dead Lake. I would never see it again and it was the end.

Sir Kato came and stood before us and his evilness nearly smothered me, since he was so close.

"What should I do now with these enemies of mine?" said Sir Kato. "What should I do with these enemies who have traveled so far to kill me? I could turn them into birds and let them fly over the Dead Lake to wail for thousands and thousands of years." He gazed at us with cruel eyes, as he pondered our fate.

"Yes, I could turn them into birds," he said. "Or—I could rip out their hearts and give them hearts of stone.

I could make them my little servants, if I give them hearts of stone."

"Oh, I'd rather be a bird," I almost shouted to him. Because I thought nothing could be worse than to have a heart of stone. But I said nothing. I knew that if I asked to be a bird, Sir Kato would give me a heart of stone.

Sir Kato looked up and down at us with his cruel eyes.

"Or I could throw them in the tower to die of hunger," he said. "I have enough birds, I have enough servants. I think I'll throw these prisoners into the tower and let them die of hunger."

He walked a few steps forward and then back across the floor, thinking deeply, and each thought made the air thicker with evil.

"In my castle you will die of hunger in a single night," he said. "In my castle, the night is so long and the hunger so great, that you will die in a single night."

He stopped before me and put his horrible claw of iron on my shoulder.

"I knew it was you, Prince Mio," he said. "I knew you had come the moment I saw your white colt. I sat here and waited for you. And you came. You believed this would be the night of our battle."

He bent down and hissed in my ear, "You thought this would be the night of our battle, but you were

wrong Prince Mio. This is your night of hunger. And
when the night is over, only small white bones will lay
in my tower. That's all that will be left of Prince Mio
and his squire."

He pounded his iron claw on a large stone table in
the middle of the floor, and a line of spies came in.

"Throw them into the tower!" he said as he pointed
to us with his iron claw. "Throw them in the tower
with seven locks! Put seven spies to guard the door, put
seventy-seven spies to guard the halls and stairs and
corridors between the tower and my room."

He sat down at the table.

"I will sit here in peace to plan my evil deeds, with
no more disruptions from Prince Mio. When the night
is over I will go and take a glance at the small white
bones in my tower. Farewell, Prince Mio! Sleep well in
my Tower of Hunger!"

The spies seized Pompoo and me and took us
through the halls of the castle to the tower, where we
were to die. And everywhere, in all of the halls and
corridors, the spies guarded the path between the tower
and Sir Kato's room. Was he so scared of me, Sir Kato,
that he needed so many guards? Was he so scared of me
without my sword, behind seven locks, and with seven
guards outside the door?

The spies held our arms tightly as we walked toward
our prison. We walked and walked through the dark,

massive castle. In one place we passed a barred window, and through the window we could see into the courtyard of the castle. In the middle of the courtyard stood a horse chained to a pole. It was a black horse with a

small black foal at its side. It hurt me to see the horses. It made me think of Miramis, whom I would never see again, and I wondered what they had done to him. Maybe he was dead. But a spy pulled my arm and forced me on and I had no more time to think of Miramis.

Mio, My Son

We reached the tower where we would spend our last night. The heavy iron doors opened and we were thrown in. The doors shut behind us with a crash, and we heard the spies turn the keys in seven locks. We were alone in our prison, Pompoo and I.

It was a round room, our prison, with thick stone walls. There was a little hole set with strong iron bars, and through these bars we heard the Bewitched Birds wail over the Dead Lake.

We sat on the floor. We felt so small and frightened, and knew we would die before the night was over.

"If only it weren't so hard to die," said Pompoo. "If only it weren't so hard, so hard to die and that we weren't so small and alone."

We held each other's hands. Tight, so tight we held each other's hands, as we sat on the cold stone floor. Hunger came over us, and it was a hunger unlike any other hunger. It gnawed at us, and tore and pulled at us draining away every ounce of strength from our blood. We wanted to sleep and never wake again. But we fought against sleep. We tried to remain awake as long as we could and began to talk of Farawayland, while we waited to die.

I thought of my father the King and tears came to my eyes. But hunger had already made me so weak and the tears flowed silently down my cheek. Pompoo cried too, quietly like I did.

"If only Farawayland weren't such a long way from here," whispered Pompoo. "If only Greenfields Island weren't so far and we weren't so small and alone."

"Do you remember when we played our flutes, walking over the hills of Greenfields Island?" I said. "Do you remember it, Pompoo?"

"Yes, but it was so long ago," said Pompoo.

"We can play our flutes here, too," I said. "We can play the old melody, until hunger overtakes us and we fall asleep."

"Yes, let's play once more," whispered Pompoo.

We took out our flutes. Our tired hands scarcely had the strength to grasp them, but we played the old melody. Pompoo cried so much as he played, tears ran quietly down his cheeks. Maybe I cried as much, I don't know. The old melody was beautiful, but sounded so faint, as if it knew that before long it would also die. Although we played quietly, the Bewitched Birds heard us. They heard the faint notes and flew over to our small window. Through the bars I saw their blank, melancholy eyes. But the birds disappeared and we had no strength to continue playing.

"Now we've played for the last time," I said as I stuffed the flute back in my pocket.

There was something else in my pocket and I stuck my hand down to feel what it was. It was the little spoon that had belonged to Totty's sister.

I wished the Bewitched Birds would come back, so I could show them the spoon. Perhaps Totty's sister would recognize it. But the Bewitched Birds were no longer in front of our small window.

I let the spoon fall to the floor, since my hand was so tired.

"Look, Pompoo," I said. "We have a spoon."

"We have a spoon," said Pompoo, "but what will we do with the spoon, when we have no food?"

Pompoo lay down on the floor and shut his eyes. He had no strength to say more. I was tired, so tired. I ached for something to eat. Anything, absolutely anything would do, as long as it was edible. Most of all I longed for the Bread That Satisfies Hunger, but I knew that I would never taste it again. I was also thirsty and longed for water from the Well That Quenches Thirst. But I knew that I would never drink again. Never drink, never eat again. I thought about the porridge that Aunt Hulda had given me every morning which I thought was bad. I would've eaten that porridge now and thought that it was good. Oh, I wanted something to eat…anything! With my last ounce of strength I grabbed the spoon and stuffed it in my mouth and pretended that I ate.

I felt something wonderful in my mouth. There was something in the spoon to eat. Something that tasted like the Bread That Satisfies Hunger and like the water from the Well That Quenches Thirst. Bread and water were in the spoon and it had the most wonderful taste. It replenished my strength and my hunger disappeared. Strangely enough, the spoon did not become empty. It filled completely with more food each time I ate, and I ate until I could eat no more.

Pompoo lay on the floor with his eyes shut. I placed the spoon in his mouth and he ate in his sleep. He lay there with his eyes shut and ate. When he finished, he said, "Oh, Mio, I had such a wonderful dream. The dream will make it easier to die. I dreamed of the Bread That Satisfies Hunger."

"It wasn't a dream," I said.

Pompoo opened his eyes and sat up. He knew that he still lived and was no longer hungry. We were both amazed, almost content in our misery.

"But what will Sir Kato do with us, since we haven't died of hunger?" said Pompoo.

"If only he doesn't give us hearts of stone," I said. "I'm afraid of having a heart of stone. I think it would grind painfully in my chest."

"The night isn't over," said Pompoo. "Sir Kato won't be here for hours. Let's sit here and talk of Farawayland, as the hours go by. Let's sit close together and keep each other warm."

It was so cold in the tower and we were freezing. My cloak slipped off. It was lying on the floor and I grabbed it and wrapped it around myself. My cloak that the Weaver had lined with fairy cloth.

That instant I heard a cry from Pompoo, "Mio! Mio, where are you?"

"I'm here," I said. "By the door."

Pompoo held up the small candle we'd been given for light during our final night. It shone in every direction and he looked so scared, totally scared.

"I can't see you," said Pompoo, "and I haven't become blind because I see the door with its strong lock and everything else in our prison."

Then I noticed I had put my cloak on inside out.

The shimmering fairy cloth lining that the Weaver had given me was turned outwards. I took off my cloak to turn it the right way and Pompoo cried out.

"Don't scare me like that again," he said. "Where were you hiding?"

"Do you see me now?" I asked.

"Of course I see you," said Pompoo. "Where were you hiding?"

"In my cloak," I said. "The Weaver must've turned it into an Invisibility Cloak."

We tried it several times. Whenever the fairy cloth lining was on the outside, my cloak became an Invisibility Cloak.

"Let's yell as loud as we can," said Pompoo. "Maybe the spies will come in to see why we're shouting. Then you can sneak past them. You can sneak out of Sir Kato's castle in your Invisibility Cloak and go home safely to Farawayland."

"And you, Pompoo?" I said.

"I must stay behind," said Pompoo and his voice quavered slightly. "You only have one Invisibility Cloak."

"I only have one Invisibility Cloak," I said, "and I only have one friend. We'll die together if we both can't be saved."

Pompoo put his arm around me and said, "I'd love for you to be safe at home in Farawayland, but I'm glad you want to stay with me. I can't help it."

Just as he said that, something strange happened. The Bewitched Birds were heading back, as their wings beat swiftly towards our window. They held something with their beaks. All the birds helped carry it. It was something heavy. It was a sword. It was my sword that could cut through stone.

"Oh, Mio," said Pompoo, "the Bewitched Birds have brought your sword up from the bottom of the Dead Lake."

I sprang to the window, stuck my eager hands through the bars and grasped my sword. It blazed as if on fire. The water flowed down, the drops glistening like fire.

"Thank you all, kind birds," I said.

But the birds only stared at me with blank, melancholy eyes and they flew with sad cries back over the Dead Lake.

"Oh, I'm so glad we played our flutes," said Pompoo. "Or the birds would've never found the way to our tower."

I hardly heard him. I stood there with the sword in my hand. My sword, my Flame of Fire! I felt so strong, as never before in my life. There was a rush and a roar inside my head. I thought of my father the King, and knew he was thinking of me.

"Now, Pompoo," I said, "now comes Sir Kato's last battle."

I Never Saw a More Fearsome Sword

Pompoo became so pale and his eyes glittered strangely.

"How will you open the seven locks?" he said. "How will you get past the seventy-seven spies?"

"I'll open the seven locks with my sword," I said. "My cloak will hide me from the seventy-seven spies."

I hung the cloak over my shoulders. The fairy cloth shimmered in the darkness, it shimmered enough to light up Sir Kato's whole castle. But Pompoo said, "I can't see you Mio, though I know you are there. I'll wait for you, until you come back."

"If I come back," I said. I kept silent, because of course I didn't know who would triumph in Sir Kato's last battle.

It was so quiet in our cell. For a long time it was completely silent. Then Pompoo said, "If you never come back, Mio, we'll think of each other. We'll think of each other as long as we can."

"Yes, Pompoo," I said. "I'll think of you and my father the King to my last moment."

I raised my sword and it slashed through the iron door as if it were made of clay. To a sword that could cut through stone, an iron door was nothing but clay. Noiselessly, as if I were cutting through clay, my sword sliced through the hard iron. Then with two quick strokes, I cut away the huge locks.

I opened the door. It creaked a little. The seven

spies stood guard outside. They all turned toward the door as it creaked. Toward the door and toward me. I stood there in my shimmering fairy cloth and thought the light around it was so bright that they must see me.

"I heard a creak in the night," said one of the spies.

"Yes, something creaked in the night," said another.

The spies peered in every direction, but didn't see me.

"It was probably an evil thought from Sir Kato that squeaked past," said another of the spies.

But I was already long gone.

I grasped my sword and I grasped my cloak and I ran as fast as I could toward Sir Kato's room.

Everywhere, in the halls, the stairs and the corridors, the spies stood guard. The entire dark, massive castle was full of black spies. But they didn't see me. They didn't hear me. And I ran on toward Sir Kato's room.

I was no longer scared. I have never been less frightened. I was not the Mio who built huts in the Garden of Roses and lived on Greenfields Island. I was a knight preparing for battle. And I ran on toward Sir Kato's room.

I ran quickly. My fairy cloak rippled behind me. It shimmered and fluttered in the dark castle. And I ran on toward Sir Kato's room.

The sword burned like fire in my hand, it flashed

brilliantly. I grasped the hilt firmly. And I ran on
toward Sir Kato's room.

I thought of my father the King. I know that he
thought about me. Soon, soon the battle draws near. I
wasn't scared. I was a knight without fear, with a sword
in my hand. And I ran on toward Sir Kato's room.

There was a rushing and roaring in my head like a
waterfall. I stood before the door to Sir Kato's room.

I opened the door. Sir Kato was sitting at his stone
table, with his back toward me. There was an evil glow
around him.

"Turn around Sir Kato," I said. "It is time for your
last battle."

He turned around. I tore off my cloak and stood before him with the sword in my hand. His awful face was gray and wrinkled. His terrible eyes were filled with terror and hatred. Quickly he gripped the sword that lay on the table beside him. So began Sir Kato's last battle.

His sword was fearsome. But no sword was as fearsome as mine. My sword flashed, it blazed and flamed, it shot through the air like fire, showing no mercy to Sir Kato.

The battle that had been foretold for thousands and thousands of years lasted an hour. My sword, the Flame of Fire, swept through the air finally striking Sir Kato's sword from his hand. Sir Kato stood before me without a weapon and he knew the battle was over.

He tore open his black velvet coat, baring his chest. "You must pierce my heart!" he shrieked. "You must slash straight through my heart of stone! It has grated so long and hurts so much."

I looked into his eyes and saw something strange. I saw that Sir Kato longed to be rid of his heart of stone. Maybe no one hated Sir Kato more than Sir Kato hated himself.

I waited no longer. I lifted my flaming sword, I lifted it high and I sank it deep into Sir Kato's terrible heart of stone.

In the blink of an eye Sir Kato vanished. He was

gone. But on the floor lay a pile of stones. Only a pile of stones and a claw of iron.

On the window sill in Sir Kato's room sat a small gray bird, pecking on the pane. It wanted out. I hadn't noticed the bird before, and didn't know where it could have been hiding. I walked to the window and opened it, so the bird could fly out. It soared into the sky, singing happily. It had been kept in captivity long enough.

I remained at the window, watching the bird fly away. And I saw that night was over and that morning had come.

Mio, My Son

YES, MORNING HAD come and it was beautiful. The sun was shining and a gentle summer breeze ruffled my hair as I stood by the open window. I leaned out and looked down over the lake. It was a cheerful blue lake, reflecting the sunshine. The Bewitched Birds were gone.

Oh, what a beautiful day! It was the kind of day when you want to play outside. I watched the water, rippled by the morning wind. I felt like throwing something into the lake, as you almost always do when you see water, and think of the splash there would be from such a height. I had nothing to throw except my sword, so I let it fall. I enjoyed watching it fall through the air, and hearing the splash as the sword hit the water. There were big rings where the sword disappeared, which became larger and larger, spreading across the lake.

But I didn't have time to stay and watch the rings die away. I had to hurry back to Pompoo. I knew he was waiting anxiously for me.

I ran back the same way I had come an hour earlier. The large halls and long corridors were empty and silent. Not a single black spy remained. The sun was shining in the deserted halls. It shone through barred windows on spider webs hanging under the arches, and you could see what a miserable old castle it was.

It was desolate and silent everywhere, and suddenly I was frightened that Pompoo might be gone too. I started to run faster and faster. But when I approached the tower, I heard Pompoo playing his flute and I laughed out loud.

I opened the door of our prison and there on the floor sat Pompoo. His eyes sparkled when he saw me, and he ran over and said, "I had to keep on playing. I was so worried."

"Now you don't have to worry any more," I said.

We were so happy, Pompoo and I. We kept looking at each other, and we laughed!

"We're leaving now," I said. "We're leaving now and we'll never come back."

We held hands and ran out of Sir Kato's castle. We ran into the castle courtyard. And who came galloping toward me, none other than Miramis! My Miramis

with the golden mane! Close by his side leaped a little white foal.

Miramis came straight toward me and I put my arms around his neck and held his beautiful head next to mine for a long, long time as I whispered in his ear, "Miramis, my own Miramis!"

Miramis looked at me with his faithful eyes, and I knew that he had longed for me as much as I had longed for him.

A pole stood in the center of the courtyard with a chain lying beside it. Then I understood that Miramis had also been bewitched. He was the black horse that had been chained in the courtyard during the night. The little foal was none other than the one Sir Kato had stolen away from the Forest of Moonbeams. It was for this little foal that the hundred white horses had wept tears of blood. Now they didn't need to cry any more, soon they would have their little foal back again.

"But what about all the others that Sir Kato has captured?" said Pompoo. "The Bewitched Birds, where have they gone?"

"Let's ride down to the lake and search for them," I said.

We climbed up on Miramis's back and the little foal followed as fast as he could. Out through the castle gates we rode.

At that moment we heard a strange and frightening noise, a rumble behind us that shook the entire ground. Sir Kato's castle had collapsed, becoming a huge pile of stones. No tower, no deserted halls, no dark winding stairs, no barred windows, nothing. Only a huge pile of stones.

"Sir Kato's castle is gone forever," said Pompoo.

"Now it's nothing but stone," I said.

A steep, twisting path ran down from the cliff toward the lake. A steep, narrow and dangerous path. But

Miramis trod carefully and placed his hooves perfectly on the path, as did the little foal. We reached the shore unhurt.

At the foot of the cliff a group of children was gathered around a slab of rock. They had certainly been waiting for us, because they came toward us with beaming faces.

"Oh! There are Nonno's brothers," said Pompoo. "There is Totty's little sister and all the others. They aren't Bewitched Birds anymore."

We hopped off Miramis. All the children came up to us, they seemed a bit shy but friendly and happy at the same time. A boy, one of Nonno's brothers, took my hand and said very quietly, as if he didn't want anyone

to hear, "I'm so glad you had my cloak to wear, and I'm so glad we're not bewitched any more."

A girl, she was Totty's sister, came up to us too. She didn't look at me, she looked out at the lake, because she was shy and she said with a soft voice, "I'm so glad that you had my spoon, and I'm so glad we're not bewitched any more."

Then another of Nonno's brothers placed his hand on my shoulder and said, "I'm so glad we could raise your sword from the depths, and I'm so glad we're not bewitched any more."

"The sword is at the bottom of the lake again," I said. "It's just as well, because I'll never need another sword."

"We will never be able to raise it again," said Nonno's brother, "because we are no longer Bewitched Birds."

I looked around, among all the children. "Which of you is the Weaver's little daughter?" I asked.

It was completely quiet. No one said a word.

"Who is the Weaver's little daughter?" I asked them again, because I wanted to tell her that my cloak was lined with the fairy cloth her mother had woven.

"Milimani was the Weaver's little daughter," said Nonno's brother.

"Where is she?" I said.

"Milimani lies there," said Nonno's brother. The children stood aside. Down at the water's edge, on the slab of rock, lay a small girl. I ran over and knelt down beside her. She lay still with her eyes closed. She was dead. Her face was so pale and small, and her body was burned.

"She flew into the torch," said Nonno's brother.

I was heartbroken. Milimani had died for my sake. I was so unhappy, nothing would ever be filled with joy again, since Milimani had died to save me.

"Don't be sad," said Nonno's brother. "Milimani wanted to do it. She wanted to fly into the torch, although she knew her wings would burn."

"But now she's dead," I said, in despair.

Nonno's brother took Milimani's small singed hands in his. "We must leave you here, Milimani," he said. "But before we go, we'll sing our song for you."

All the children sat down on the rock around Milimani and sang her a song they had made up.

"Milimani, our little sister,
little sister who went down in the waves,
went down in the waves with singed wings.
Milimani, oh, Milimani
sleeps quietly and never wakes,
never again flies Milimani
with sorrowful cries over the murky water."

"It isn't murky water anymore," said Pompoo. "There are only small gentle waves that sing to Milimani as she lies sleeping on the shore."

"If only we had something to wrap around her," said Totty's sister. "Something soft so that she doesn't have to lie on the hard rock."

"We'll wrap Milimani in my cloak," I said. "We'll wrap her in the cloth that her mother wove."

I wrapped Milimani in my cloak which was lined with fairy cloth. It was softer than apple blossoms, gentler than the night wind in the grass, warmer than a beating heart and her own mother had woven it. I carefully wrapped my cloak around Milimani, so she would lay softly on the rock.

Then something strange happened. Milimani opened up her eyes and looked at me. At first she lay still, just watching me. Then she sat up, staring in astonishment at all the children. She kept glancing around, in more and more amazement.

"How blue the lake is," she said.

That was all she said. Then she took off the cloak and stood up; there were no traces of her burns and we were overjoyed that she was alive again.

Out on the water a boat glided toward us. Someone rowed, taking huge strokes at the oars. As the boat approached, I saw the Swordsmith was rowing and he had Eno with him.

Soon their boat bumped against the rock and they jumped ashore.

"What did I say?" bellowed the Swordsmith. "What

did I say? 'Sir Kato's final battle approaches.' That's what I said."

Eno eagerly drew near me. "I want to show you something, Prince Mio," he said.

He held out his wrinkled hand to show me what was in it. It was a small green leaf. Such a fine little leaf it was, thin and soft and perfectly light green, with slender veins.

"It was growing in the Dead Forest," said Eno. "I found it on a tree in the Dead Forest, just now."

He nodded in satisfaction, his gray head bobbing up and down.

"I will go out in the Dead Forest each morning to check for more green leaves," he said. "You can have this one, Prince Mio."

He placed the leaf in my hand and certainly thought that he was giving away the finest gift of all.

Then he nodded again and said, "I sat and wished you well, Prince Mio. I sat there in my cottage and wished you well."

"What did I say?" said the Swordsmith. "I said, 'Sir Kato's final battle approaches.'"

"How did you get your boat back?" I asked the Swordsmith.

"The waves carried it across the lake," said the Swordsmith.

I glanced over the lake toward the Swordsmith's

mountain and Eno's cottage. More boats appeared on the water, filled with people I'd never seen before. These small, pale people gazed at the sun and the blue lake in wonder. I don't think they'd ever seen the sun before, which was shining brightly on the lake and over the rocks. It was so lovely. Only the big pile of stones up on the cliff wasn't pretty. But I thought that one day moss would grow over the pile of stones. It would be hidden under the soft, green moss and no one would know that underneath lay Sir Kato's castle.

I've seen a pink flower that likes to grow on moss. It looks like a small, small bell that grows on long tendrils. In time, maybe, there will be small pink bells on the moss covering Sir Kato's castle. It'll be pretty enough, I think.

The way home was long, but walking was easy. The small children rode on Miramis, and the very smallest rode on the foal. They thought it was fun. The rest of us continued on foot, until we came to the Forest of Moonbeams.

By then it had become night and the Forest of Moonbeams was filled with moonlight, just as before. It was quiet among the trees. But Miramis neighed so loudly and wildly, and deep in the Forest of Moonbeams the hundred white horses answered just as loudly and wildly. They came galloping toward us, their hooves thundering over the ground. The little foal also began

to neigh. He tried to neigh loudly and wildly like the bigger horses, but it was only a faint little amusing whinny that you could hardly hear. But the hundred white horses definitely heard it. Oh, how glad they were the little foal had come home! They crowded around him, they all tried to get near and touch him to make sure he had really come home.

Now we had the hundred horses and no one needed to walk on foot. All the children had horses to ride. I rode on Miramis and Pompoo sat behind me, as always, because he wouldn't ride any other horse but Miramis. A little girl, who was the smallest of all, got to ride the foal.

We rode through the forest, and the hundred white horses looked so pretty in the moonlight.

Soon I saw something white shining between the trees, the apple blossoms around the Weaver's cottage. The apple blossoms lay on the trees in a soft drift, around the cottage that looked as if it was from a fairy tale. We heard a pounding noise inside, and Milimani said, "My mother sits and weaves."

She jumped off her horse just outside the gate, and waved to us and said, "I'm so glad to be home. I'm so glad to be home before the apple trees stopped blooming."

She ran down the little path between the trees and disappeared into the cottage. The pounding stopped inside.

We still had a long way to go to reach Greenfields Island, and I longed for it and for my father the King. The hundred white horses, led by Miramis, rose over the Forest of Moonbeams, high over the tall mountains and they flew through the air on the way to Greenfields Island.

It was morning when we came to the Bridge of Morninglight. The guards had just lowered the bridge, which shone with golden rays of light, as the hundred white horses, with necks stretched and manes flowing, galloped across it. The guards stared at us in amazement. Suddenly one of them pulled out a horn and blew it so loudly that it rang across Greenfields Island. People came running from all the small houses and cottages, those who had mourned and grieved for their lost children. Now they saw us come riding up on white horses and no one was missing. All had come home.

The white horses galloped on over the fields and soon we came to my father the King's garden. All of the children jumped down, their mamas and papas came running and they carried on as the hundred white horses had when their foal came home. Nonno was there too, and his grandmother, and Totty with his sisters and brothers, and Pompoo's mama and papa and many other people I'd never seen before. They cried and laughed together, and hugged and kissed the children who had come home.

But my father the King was not there.

We didn't need the hundred white horses any more, so they turned back to the Forest of Moonbeams. I saw them gallop away over the fields. In front of them all ran the little white foal.

Pompoo was telling his mama and papa all that we had been through and he didn't notice that I opened the little door to the Garden of Roses. No one noticed when I disappeared into the Garden of Roses, and that was fine. I wanted to go alone. I walked under the silver poplars playing their music just as they had before, the roses bloomed just as they had before, everything was the same.

Then I saw him. I saw my father the King. He stood in the same place, where I had left him when I rode away to the Forest of Moonbeams and to Outer Land. He stood there with his arms outstretched to me and I threw myself into his embrace. I put my arms tightly, so tightly around his neck and he held me close and whispered, "Mio, my son!"

My father the King loves me, and I love my father the King.

I had so much fun the whole day. We played in the Garden of Roses, Pompoo and Nonno and his brothers, and Totty and his sisters and brothers, and all the other children. They wanted to see the hut that we had built, Pompoo and I, and they thought it was such a fine hut. We rode on Miramis too, and he jumped over the rose bushes. We played with my cloak. Nonno's brother didn't want it back.

"The lining is yours anyway, Mio," he said.

We played hide-and-seek with the cloak. I was wearing it inside out and I ran around among the rose bushes completely invisible, shouting, "No one can catch me! No one can catch me!"

And they couldn't catch me either, as hard as they tried.

When it began to get dark, all the children had to go home. Their mamas and papas didn't want them out for a long time, since it was their first night home.

Pompoo and I sat together, alone in our hut. We played our flutes as twilight fell over the Garden of Roses.

"We'll take care of our flutes," said Pompoo. "And if we ever become separated, we'll play the old melody."

Just then my father the King came to find me. I said good night to Pompoo and he ran home. I said good night to Miramis, as he grazed on the grass beside the hut. Then I took my father the King's hand and we walked home through the Garden of Roses.

"Mio, my son, I believe that you've grown while you were away," said my father the King. "I think we should put a new mark on the kitchen door tonight."

We walked under the silver poplars as twilight lay like a soft, blue mist over the entire Garden of Roses. The white birds had gone to their nests. In the top of the tallest silver poplar Sorrowbird sat singing. I don't know what the song is for, now that the lost children have come home. But I think Sorrowbird will always have something to sing about.

Away in the pastures, shepherds began lighting their fires. One by one they appeared, shining beautifully in the twilight. Far away I heard the shepherds playing. They played the old melody.

We walked along hand in hand, my father the King

and I, swinging our arms a bit. My father the King looked down at me and laughed a little, and I looked up at him, full of happiness.

"Mio, my son," said my father the King.

No more.

"Mio, my son," said my father the King, as we walked homeward in the twilight.

Evening came and then night.

It's been quite a long time now that I've been here in Farawayland. I seldom think of the time when I lived on North Street. It's only Ben that I think of sometimes, because he's so much like Pompoo. I hope Ben hasn't missed me too much. Because no one knows better than I do how hard it is to be lonely. But of course Ben has his mama and papa, and by now I think he probably has a new best friend.

Sometimes I also think about Aunt Hulda and Uncle Olaf and I'm not angry at them anymore. I only wonder about what they said when I disappeared. They never worried about me, maybe they didn't even notice I was gone. Maybe Aunt Hulda believes that she only has to go to Tegnérlunden Park to look, and she'd find me sitting on a bench. Maybe she believes that I'm sitting there on a bench under a street lamp, eating an apple and playing with an empty bottle or some other piece of rubbish. Maybe she believes that I'm sitting there,

175

staring at the houses with lighted windows and children inside eating dinner with their mamas and papas. Maybe Aunt Hulda is angry that I never came home with those rolls.

But Aunt Hulda is wrong. Oh, she is wrong! Andy isn't sitting on a bench in Tegnérlunden Park, because he's in Farawayland. *He is in Farawayland, I say.* He's where the silver poplars rustle…where fires burn warming the night…where there is Bread That Satisfies Hunger…where he has his father the King, whom he loves so much and who loves him.

Yes, so it is. Karl Anders Nilsson is in Farawayland and all is fine, so fine with his father the King.

TITLES IN THE
NEW YORK REVIEW CHILDREN'S COLLECTION

ESTHER AVERILL
Captains of the City Streets
The Hotel Cat
Jenny and the Cat Club
Jenny Goes to Sea
Jenny's Birthday Book
Jenny's Moonlight Adventure
The School for Cats

JAMES CLOYD BOWMAN
Pecos Bill: The Greatest Cowboy of All Time

PALMER BROWN
Beyond the Pawpaw Trees
Cheerful
Hickory
The Silver Nutmeg
Something for Christmas

SHEILA BURNFORD
Bel Ria: Dog of War

DINO BUZZATI
The Bears' Famous Invasion of Sicily

MARY CHASE
Loretta Mason Potts

CARLO COLLODI and FULVIO TESTA
Pinocchio

INGRI and EDGAR PARIN D'AULAIRE
D'Aulaires' Book of Animals
D'Aulaires' Book of Norse Myths
D'Aulaires' Book of Trolls
Foxie: The Singing Dog
The Terrible Troll-Bird
Too Big
The Two Cars

EILÍS DILLON
The Island of Horses
The Lost Island

ELEANOR FARJEON
The Little Bookroom

PENELOPE FARMER
Charlotte Sometimes

PAUL GALLICO
The Abandoned

LEON GARFIELD
The Complete Bostock and Harris
Smith: The Story of a Pickpocket

RUMER GODDEN
An Episode of Sparrows
The Mousewife

MARIA GRIPE and HARALD GRIPE
The Glassblower's Children

LUCRETIA P. HALE
The Peterkin Papers

RUSSELL and LILLIAN HOBAN
The Sorely Trying Day

RUTH KRAUSS and MARC SIMONT
The Backward Day

DOROTHY KUNHARDT
Junket Is Nice
Now Open the Box

MUNRO LEAF and ROBERT LAWSON
Wee Gillis

RHODA LEVINE and EDWARD GOREY
He Was There from the Day We Moved In
Three Ladies Beside the Sea